IF BEALE STREET COULD TALK

"To be James Baldwin is to touch on so many hidden places in Europe, in America, the Negro, the white man—to be forced to understand so much."

—Alfred Kazin

"This author retains a place in an extremely select group: that composed of the few genuinely indispensable American writers."

—*Saturday Review*

"He has not himself lost access to the sources of his being—which is what makes him read and awaited by perhaps a wider range of people than any other major American writer."

—*The Nation*

"He is thought-provoking, tantalizing, irritating, abusing and amusing. And he uses words as the sea uses waves, to flow and beat, advance and retreat, rise and take a bow in disappearing ... the thought becomes poetry and the poetry illuminates the thought."

—Langston Hughes

"He has become one of the few writers of our time."

—Norman Mailer

OTHER DELL TITLES BY JAMES BALDWIN:

THE AMEN CORNER

ANOTHER COUNTRY

BLUES FOR MISTER CHARLIE

THE DEVIL FINDS WORK

THE FIRE NEXT TIME

GIOVANNI'S ROOM

GO TELL IT ON THE MOUNTAIN

GOING TO MEET THE MAN

IF BEALE STREET COULD TALK

JUST ABOVE MY HEAD

NO NAME IN THE STREET

NOBODY KNOWS MY NAME

ONE DAY, WHEN I WAS LOST

TELL ME HOW LONG THE TRAIN'S BEEN GONE

IF
BEALE
STREET
COULD TALK

JAMES BALDWIN

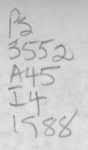
A LAUREL BOOK
Published by
Dell Publishing
a division of
Bantam Doubleday Dell
Publishing Group, Inc.
666 Fifth Avenue
New York, New York 10103

Front cover photograph: Stuart Gross

The lines on page 113 are from "My Man," words by Albert Willemetz and
Jacques Charles, music by Maurice Yvain, English lyric by Channing
Pollock. Copyright 1920 by Francis Salabert, Paris, France. Copyright
renewal 1948 Francis Salabert, Paris, France. Copyright renewal 1949
Francis Salabert, Paris, France—Leo Feist, Inc., New York, N.Y. Used by
permission.

ISBN: 0-440-34060-8

Printed in the United States of America
Published simultaneously in Canada
Reprinted by arrangement with Doubleday & Company, Inc.
Two previous editions
May 1988
10   9   8   7

RAD

for YORAN

Mary, Mary,
   What you going to name
   That pretty little baby?

ONE

Troubled About My Soul

I look at myself in the mirror. I know that I was christened Clementine, and so it would make sense if people called me Clem, or even, come to think of it, Clementine, since that's my name: but they don't. People call me Tish. I guess that makes sense, too. I'm tired, and I'm beginning to think that maybe everything that happens makes sense. Like, if it didn't make sense, how could it happen? But that's really a terrible thought. It can only come out of trouble—trouble that doesn't make sense.

Today, I went to see Fonny. That's not *his* name, either, he was christened Alonzo: and it might make sense if people called him Lonnie. But, no, we've always called him Fonny. Alonzo Hunt, that's his name. I've known him all my life, and I hope I'll always know him. But I only call him Alonzo when I have to break down some real heavy shit to him.

Today, I said, "—Alonzo—?"

And he looked at me, that quickening look he has when I call him by his name.

He's in jail. So where we were, I was sitting on a bench in front of a board, and he was sitting on a bench in front of a board. And we were facing each other through a wall of glass between us. You can't hear anything through this glass, and so you both have a little telephone. You have to talk through that. I don't know why people always look down when they talk through a telephone, but they always do. You have to remember to look up at the person you're talking to.

I always remember now, because he's in jail and I love his eyes and every time I see him I'm afraid I'll never see him again. So I pick up the phone as soon as I get there and I just hold it and I keep looking up at him.

So, when I said, "—Alonzo—?" he looked down and then he looked up and he smiled and he held the phone and he waited.

I hope that nobody has ever had to look at anybody they love through glass.

And I didn't say it the way I meant to say it. I meant to say it in a very offhand way, so he wouldn't be too upset, so he'd understand that I was saying it without any kind of accusation in my heart.

You see: I know him. He's very proud, and he worries a lot, and, when I think about it, I know—he doesn't— that that's the biggest reason he's in jail. He worries too much already, I don't want him to worry about me. In fact, I didn't want to say what I had to say. But I knew I had to say it. He had to know.

And I thought, too, that when he got over being worried, when he was lying by himself at night, when he was all by himself, in the very deepest part of himself, maybe, when he thought about it, he'd be glad. And that might help him.

I said, "Alonzo, we're going to have a baby."

I looked at him. I know I smiled. His face looked as though it were plunging into water. I couldn't touch him. I wanted so to touch him. I smiled again and my hands got wet on the phone and then for a moment I couldn't see him at all and I shook my head and my face was wet and I said, "I'm glad. I'm glad. Don't you worry. I'm glad."

But he was far away from me now, all by himself. I waited for him to come back. I could see it flash across his face: *my* baby? I knew that he would think that. I don't mean that he doubted *me*: but a man thinks that. And for those few seconds while he was out there by himself, away from me, the baby was the only real thing in the world, more real than the prison, more real than me.

I should have said already: we're not married. That means more to him than it does to me, but I understand how he feels. We were going to get married, but then he went to jail.

Fonny is twenty-two. I am nineteen.

He asked the ridiculous question: "Are you sure?"

"No. I ain't sure. I'm just trying to mess with your mind."

Then he grinned. He grinned because, then, he knew.

"What we going to do?" he asked me—just like a little boy.

"Well, we ain't going to drown it. So, I guess we'll have to raise it."

Fonny threw back his head, and laughed, he laughed till tears come down his face. So, then, I felt that the first part, that I'd been so frightened of, would be all right.

"Did you tell Frank?" he asked me.

Frank is his father.

I said, "Not yet."

"You tell your folks?"

"Not yet. But don't worry about them. I just wanted to tell you first."

"Well," he said, "I guess that makes sense. A baby." He looked at me, then he looked down. "What you going to do, for real?"

"I'm going to do just like I been doing. I'll work up to just about the last month. And then, Mama and Sis will take care for me, you ain't got to worry. And anyway we have you out of here before then."

"You sure about that?" With his little smile.

"Of course I'm sure about that. I'm always sure about that."

I knew what he was thinking, but I can't let myself think about it—not now, watching him. I *must* be sure.

The man came up behind Fonny, and it was time to go. Fonny smiled and raised his fist, like always, and I raised mine and he stood up. I'm always kind of surprised when I see him in here, at how tall he is. Of course, he's lost weight and that may make him seem taller.

He turned around and went through the door and the door closed behind him.

I felt dizzy. I hadn't eaten much all day, and now it was getting late.

I walked out, to cross these big, wide corridors I've come to hate, corridors wider than all the Sahara desert. The Sahara is never empty; these corridors are never empty. If you cross the Sahara, and you fall, by and by vultures circle around you, smelling, sensing, your death. They circle lower and lower: they wait. They know. They know exactly when the flesh is ready, when the spirit cannot fight back. The poor are always crossing the Sahara. And the lawyers and bondsmen and all that crowd circle around the poor, exactly like vultures. Of course, they're not any richer than the poor, really, that's why they've turned into vultures, scavengers, indecent garbage men, and I'm talking about the black cats, too, who, in so many ways, are worse. I think that, personally, I would be ashamed. But I've had to think about it and now I think that maybe not. I don't know what I wouldn't do to get Fonny out of jail. I've never come across any shame down here, except shame like mine, except the shame of the hardworking black ladies, who call me Daughter, and the shame of proud Puerto Ricans, who don't understand what's happened—no one who speaks to them speaks Spanish, for example—and who are ashamed that they have loved ones in jail. But they are wrong to be ashamed. The people responsible for these jails should be ashamed.

And I'm not ashamed of Fonny. If anything, I'm proud. He's a man. You can tell by the way he's taken all this shit that he's a man. Sometimes, I admit, I'm scared—because nobody can take the shit they throw on us forever. But, then, you just have to somehow fix your mind to get from one day to the next. If you think too far ahead, if you even *try* to think too far ahead, you'll never make it.

Sometimes I take the subway home, sometimes I take the bus. Today, I took the bus because it takes a little longer and I had a lot on my mind.

Being in trouble can have a funny effect on the mind. I don't know if I can explain this. You go through some days and you seem to be hearing people and you seem to be talking to them and you seem to be doing your work, or, at least, your work gets done; but you haven't seen or heard a soul and if someone asked you what you have done that day you'd have to think awhile before you could answer. But, at the same time, and even on the self-same day—and this is what is hard to explain—you see people like you never saw them before. They shine as bright as a razor. Maybe it's because you see people differently than you saw them before your trouble started. Maybe you wonder about them more, but in a different way, and this makes them very strange to you. Maybe you get scared and numb, because you don't know if you can depend on people for anything, anymore.

And, even if they wanted to do something, what could they do? I can't say to anybody in this bus, Look, Fonny is in trouble, he's in jail—can you imagine what anybody on this bus would say to me if they knew, from my mouth, that I love somebody in jail?—and I know he's never committed any crime and he's a beautiful person, please help me get him out. Can you imagine what anybody on this bus would say? What would *you* say? I can't say, I'm going to have this baby and I'm scared, too, and I don't want anything to happen to my baby's father, don't let him die in prison, please, oh, please! You can't say that. That means you can't really say anything. Trouble means you're alone. You sit down, and you look out the window and you wonder if you're going to spend the rest of your life going back and forth on this bus. And if you do, what's going to happen to your baby? What's going to happen to Fonny?

And if you ever did like the city, you don't like it anymore. If I ever get out of this, if we ever get out of this, I swear I'll never set foot in downtown New York again.

Maybe I used to like it, a long time ago, when Daddy used to bring me and Sis here and we'd watch the people and the buildings and Daddy would point out different sights to us and we might stop in Battery Park and have ice cream and hot dogs. Those were great days and we were always very happy—but that was because of our father, not because of the city. It was because we knew our father loved us. Now, I can say, because I certainly know it now, the city didn't. They looked at us as though we were zebras—and, you know, some people like zebras and some people don't. But nobody ever asks the zebra.

It's true that I haven't seen much of other cities, only Philadelphia and Albany, but I swear that New York must be the ugliest and the dirtiest city in the world. It must have the ugliest buildings and the nastiest people. It's got to have the worst cops. If any place is worse, it's got to be so close to hell that you can smell the people frying. And, come to think of it, that's exactly the smell of New York in the summertime.

I met Fonny in the streets of this city. I was little, he was not so little. I was around six—somewhere around there—and he was around nine. They lived across the street, him and his family, his mother and two older sisters and his father, and his father ran a tailor shop. Looking back, now, I kind of wonder who he ran the tailor shop *for*: we didn't know anybody who had money to take clothes to the tailor—well, maybe once in a great while. But I don't think *we* could have kept him in business. Of course, as I've been told, people, colored people, weren't as poor then as they had been when my Mama and Daddy were trying to get it together. They weren't as poor then as we had been in the South. But we were certainly poor enough, and we still are.

I never really noticed Fonny until once we got into a fight, after school. This fight didn't really have anything to do with Fonny and me at all. I had a girl friend, named Geneva, a kind of loud, raunchy girl, with her hair plaited tight on her head, with big, ashy knees and long legs and big feet; and she was always into something. Naturally she was my best friend, since I was never into anything. I was skinny and scared and so I followed her and got into all *her* shit. Nobody else wanted me, really, and you *know* that nobody else wanted her. Well, she said that she couldn't stand Fonny. Every time she looked at him, it just made her sick. She was always telling me how ugly he was, with skin just like raw, wet potato rinds and eyes like a Chinaman and all that nappy hair and them thick lips. And so bowlegged he had bunions on his ankle bones; and the way his behind stuck out, his mother must have been a gorilla. I agreed with her because I had to, but I didn't really think he was as bad as all that. I kind of liked his eyes, and, to tell the truth, I thought that if people in China had eyes like that, I wouldn't mind going to China. I had never seen a gorilla, so his behind looked perfectly normal to me, and wasn't, really, when you had to think about it, as big as Geneva's; and it wasn't until much later that I realized that he was, yes, a little bowlegged. But Geneva was always up in Fonny's face. I don't think he ever noticed her at all. He was always too busy with his friends, who were the worst boys on the block. They were always coming down the street, in rags, bleeding, full of lumps, and, just before this fight, Fonny had lost a tooth.

Fonny had a friend named Daniel, a big, black boy, and Daniel had a thing about Geneva something like the way Geneva had a thing about Fonny. And I don't remember how it all started, but, finally, Daniel had

Geneva down on the ground, the two of them rolling around, and I was trying to pull Daniel off her and Fonny was pulling on me. I turned around and hit him with the only thing I could get my hands on, I grabbed it out of the garbage can. It was only a stick; but it had a nail in it. The nail raked across his cheek and it broke the skin and the blood started dripping. I couldn't believe my eyes, I was so scared. Fonny put his hand to his face and then looked at me and then looked at his hand and I didn't have any better sense than to drop the stick and run. Fonny ran after me and, to make matters worse, Geneva saw the blood and she started screaming that I'd killed him, I'd killed him! Fonny caught up to me in no time and he grabbed me tight and he spit at me through the hole where his tooth used to be. He caught me right on the mouth, and—it so *humiliated* me, I guess—because he hadn't hit me, or hurt me—and maybe because I sensed what he had not done —that I screamed and started to cry. It's funny. Maybe my life changed in that very moment when Fonny's spit hit me in the mouth. Geneva and Daniel, who had started the whole thing, and didn't have a scratch on them, both began to scream at me. Geneva said that I'd killed him for sure, yes, I'd killed him, people caught the lockjaw and died from rusty nails. And Daniel said, Yes, he knew, he had a uncle down home who died like that. Fonny was listening to all this, while the blood kept dripping and I kept crying. Finally, he must have realized that they were talking about him, and that he was a dead man—or boy—because he started crying, too, and then Daniel and Geneva took him between them and walked off, leaving me there, alone.

And I didn't see Fonny for a couple of days. I was sure he had the lockjaw, and was dying; and Geneva said that just as soon as he was dead, which would be any minute, the police would come and put me in the electric chair. I watched the tailor shop, but everything seemed normal. Mr. Hunt was there, with his laughing, light-brown-skinned self, pressing pants, and telling jokes to whoever was in the shop—there was always someone in the shop—and every once in a while, Mrs. Hunt would come by. She was a Sanctified woman, who didn't smile much, but, still, neither of them acted as if their son was dying.

So, when I hadn't seen Fonny for a couple of days, I waited until the tailor shop seemed empty, when Mr. Hunt was in there by himself, and I went over there. Mr. Hunt knew me, then, a little, like we all knew each other on the block.

"Hey, Tish," he said, "how you doing? How's the family?"

I said, "Just fine, Mr. Hunt." I wanted to say, How's *your* family? which I always *did* say and had planned to say, but I couldn't.

"How you doing in school?" he asked me, after a minute: and I thought he looked at me in a real strange way.

"Oh, all right," I said, and my heart started to beating like it was going to jump out of my chest.

Mr. Hunt pressed down that sort of double ironing board they have in tailor shops—like two ironing boards facing each other—he pressed that down, and he looked at me for a minute and then he laughed and said, "Reckon that big-headed boy of mine be back here pretty soon."

I heard what he said, and I understood—something; but I didn't know what it was I understood.

I walked to the door of the shop, making like I was going out, and then I turned and I said, "What's that, Mr. Hunt?"

Mr. Hunt was still smiling. He pulled the presser down and turned over the pants or whatever it was he had in there, and said, "Fonny. His Mama sent him down to her folks in the country for a little while. Claim he get into too much trouble up here."

He pressed the presser down again. "She don't know what kind of trouble he like to get in down there." Then he looked up at me and he smiled. When I got to know Fonny and I got to know Mr. Hunt better, I realized that Fonny has his smile. "Oh, I'll tell him you come by," he said.

I said, "Say hello to the family for me, Mr. Hunt," and I ran across the street.

Geneva was on my stoop and she told me I looked like a fool and that I'd almost got run over.

I stopped and said, "You a liar, Geneva Braithwaite. Fonny ain't got the lockjaw and he ain't going to die. And I ain't going to jail. Now, you just go and ask his Daddy." And then Geneva gave me such a funny look that I ran up my stoop and up the stairs and I sat down on the fire escape, but sort of in the window, where she couldn't see me.

Fonny came back, about four or five days later, and he came over to my stoop. He didn't have a scar on him. He had two doughnuts. He sat down on my stoop. He said, "I'm sorry I spit in your face." And he gave me one of his doughnuts.

I said, "I'm sorry I hit you." And then we didn't say anything. He ate his doughnut and I ate mine.

People don't believe it about boys and girls that age —people don't believe much and I'm beginning to know why—but, then, we got to be friends. Or, maybe, and it's really the same thing—something else people don't want to know—I got to be his little sister and he got to be my big brother. He didn't like his sisters and I didn't have any brothers. And so we got to be, for each other, what the other missed.

Geneva got mad at me and she stopped being my friend; though, maybe, now that I think about it, without even knowing it, I stopped being *her* friend; because, now—and without knowing what that meant —I had Fonny. Daniel got mad at Fonny, he called him a sissy for fooling around with girls, and he stopped being Fonny's friend—for a long time; they even had a fight and Fonny lost another tooth. I think that anyone watching Fonny then was sure that he'd grow up without a single tooth in his head. I remember telling Fonny that I'd get my mother's scissors from upstairs and go and kill Daniel, but Fonny said I wasn't nothing but a girl and didn't have nothing to do with it.

Fonny had to go to church on Sundays—and I mean, he *had* to go: though he managed to outwit his mother more often than she knew, or cared to know. His mother—I got to know her better, too, later on, and we're going to talk about her in a minute—was, as I've said, a Sanctified woman and if she couldn't save her husband, she was damn sure going to save her child. Because it was *her* child; it wasn't *their* child.

I think that's why Fonny was so bad. And I think that's why he was, when you got to know him, so nice, a really nice person, a really sweet man, with something very sad in him: when you got to know him. Mr. Hunt, Frank, didn't try to claim him but he loved him—loves him. The two older sisters weren't Sanctified exactly, but they might as well have been, and they certainly took after their mother. So that left just Frank and Fonny. In a way, Frank had Fonny all week long, Fonny had Frank all week long. They both knew this and that was why Frank could give Fonny to his mother on Sundays. What Fonny was doing in the street was just exactly what Frank was doing in the tailor shop and in the house. He was being bad. That's why he hold on to that tailor shop as long as he could. That's why, when Fonny came home bleeding, Frank could tend to him; that's why they could, both the father and the son, love me. It's not really a mystery except it's always a mystery about people. I used to wonder, later, if Fonny's mother and father ever made love together. I asked Fonny. And Fonny said:

"Yeah. But not like you and me. I used to hear them. She'd come home from church, wringing wet and funky. She'd act like she was so tired she could hardly move and she'd just fall across the bed with her clothes on—she'd maybe had enough strength to take off her shoes. And her hat. And she'd always lay her handbag down someplace. I can still hear that sound, like something heavy, with silver inside it, dropping heavy wherever she laid it down. I'd hear her say, The Lord sure blessed my soul this evening. Honey, when you going to give your life to the Lord? And, baby, he'd say, and I swear to you he was lying there with his dick getting hard, and, excuse me, baby, but her condition weren't no better, because this, you dig? was like the game you hear two alley cats playing in the alley. Shit. She going to whelp and *mee-e-ow* till times get better, she going to get that cat, she going to run him all *over* the alley, she going run him till he bite her by the neck—by this time he just want to get some sleep really, but she got her chorus going, he's got to stop the music and ain't but one way to do it—he going to bite her by the neck and then she got him. So, my Daddy just lay there, didn't have no clothes on, with his dick getting harder and harder, and my Daddy would say, About the time, I reckon, that the Lord gives *his* life to *me*. And she'd say, Oh, Frank, let me bring you to the Lord. And he'd say, Shit, woman, I'm going to bring the Lord to *you*. *I'm* the Lord. And she'd start to crying, and she'd moan, Lord, help me help this man. You give him to me. I can't do nothing about it. Oh, Lord, help me. And he'd say, The Lord's going to help you, sugar, just as soon as you get to be a little child again, naked, like a little child. Come on, come to the Lord. And she'd start to crying and calling on Jesus while he started taking all her clothes off—I could hear them kind of rustling and whistling and tearing and falling to the floor and sometimes I'd get my foot caught in one of them things when I was coming through their room in the morning on my way to school—and when he got her naked and got on top of her and she was still crying, Jesus! help me, Lord! my Daddy would say, You got the Lord now, right here. Where you want your blessing? Where do it hurt? Where you want the Lord's hands to touch you? here? here? or here? Where you want his tongue? Where you want the Lord to enter you, you dirty, dumb black bitch? you bitch. You bitch. You bitch. And he'd slap her, hard, loud. And she'd say, Oh, Lord, help me to bear my burden. And he'd say, Here it is, baby, you going to bear it all right, I know it. You got a friend in Jesus, and I'm going to tell you when he comes. The first time. We don't know nothing about the second coming. Yet. And the bed would shake and she would moan and moan and moan. And, in the morning, was just like nothing never happened. She was just like she had been. She still belonged to Jesus and he went off down the street, to the shop."

And then Fonny said, "Hadn't been for me, I believe the cat would have split the scene. I'll always love my

Daddy because he didn't leave me." I'll always remember Fonny's face when he talked about his Daddy.

Then, Fonny would turn to me and take me in his arms and laugh and say, "You remind me a lot of my mother, you know that? Come on, now, and let's sing together, Sinner, do you love my Lord?—And if I don't hear no moaning, I'll know you ain't been saved."

I guess it can't be too often that two people can laugh and make love, too, make love because they are laughing, laugh because they're making love. The love and the laughter come from the same place: but not many people go there.

Fonny asked me, one Saturday, if I could come to church with him in the morning and I said, Yes, though we were Baptists and weren't supposed to go to a Sanctified church. But, by this time, everybody knew that Fonny and I were friends, it was just simply a fact. At school, and all up and down the block, they called us Romeo and Juliet, though this was not because they'd read the play, and here Fonny came, looking absolutely miserable, with his hair all slicked and shining, with the part in his hair so cruel that it looked like it had been put there with a tomahawk or a razor, wearing his blue suit and Sis had got me dressed and so we went. It was like, when you think about it, our first date. His mother was waiting downstairs.

It was just before Easter, so it wasn't cold but it wasn't hot.

Now, although we were little and I certainly couldn't

be dreaming of taking Fonny from her or anything like that, and although she didn't really love Fonny, only thought that she was supposed to because she had spasmed him into this world, already, Fonny's mother didn't like me. I could tell from lots of things, such as, for example, I hardly ever went to Fonny's house but Fonny was always at mine; and this wasn't because Fonny and Frank didn't want me in their house. It was because the mother and them two sisters didn't want me. In one way, as I realized later, they didn't think that I was good enough for Fonny—which really means that they didn't think that I was good enough for *them*—and in another way, they felt that I was maybe just exactly what Fonny deserved. Well, I'm dark and my hair is just plain hair and there is nothing very outstanding about me and not even Fonny bothers to pretend I'm pretty, he just says that pretty girls are a terrible drag.

When he says this, I know that he's thinking about his mother—that's why, when he wants to tease me, he tells me I remind him of his mother. I don't remind him of his mother at all, and he knows that, but he also knows that I know how much he loved her: how much he wanted to love her, to be allowed to love her, to have that translation read.

Mrs. Hunt and the girls are fair; and you could see that Mrs. Hunt had been a very beautiful girl down there in Atlanta, where she comes from. And she still had—has—that look, that don't-you-touch-me look, that women who were beautiful carry with them to the grave. The sisters weren't as beautiful as the mother and, of course, they'd never been young, in Atlanta, but they were fair skinned—and their hair was long. Fonny is lighter than me but much darker than they, his hair is just plain nappy and all the grease his mother put into it every Sunday couldn't take out the naps.

Fonny really takes after his father: so, Mrs. Hunt gave me a real sweet patient smile as Fonny brought me out the house that Sunday morning.

"I'm mighty pleased you coming to the house of the Lord this morning, Tish," she said. "My, you look pretty this morning!"

The way she said it made me *know* what I have must looked like other mornings: it made me know what I looked like.

I said, "Good-morning, Mrs. Hunt," and we started down the street.

It was the Sunday morning street. Our streets have days, and even hours. Where I was born, and where my baby will be born, you look down the street and you can almost see what's happening in the house: like, say, Saturday, at three in the afternoon, is a very bad hour. The kids are home from school. The men are home from work. You'd think that this might be a very happy get-together, but it isn't. The kids see the men. The men see the kids. And this drives the women, who are cooking and cleaning and straightening hair and who see what men won't see, almost crazy. You can see it in the streets, you can hear it in the way the women yell for their children. You can see it in the way they come down out of the house—in a rush, like a storm—and slap the children and drag them upstairs, you can hear it in the child, you can see it in the way the men, ignoring all this, stand together in front of a railing, sit together in the barbershop, pass a bottle between them, walk to the corner to the bar, tease the girl behind the bar, fight with each other, and get very busy, later, with their vines. Saturday afternoon is like a cloud hanging over, it's like waiting for a storm to break.

But, on Sunday mornings the clouds have lifted, the storm has done its damage and gone. No matter what the damage was, everybody's clean now. The women have somehow managed to get it all together, to hold everything together. So, here everybody is, cleaned, scrubbed, brushed, and greased. Later, they're going to eat ham hocks or chitterlings or fried or roasted chicken, with yams and rice and greens or cornbread or biscuits. They're going to come home and fall out and be friendly: and some men wash their cars, on Sundays, more carefully than they wash their foreskins. Walking down the street that Sunday morning, with Fonny walking beside me like a prisoner and Mrs. Hunt on the other side of me, like a queen making great strides into the kingdom, was like walking through a fair. But now I think that it was only Fonny—who didn't say a word—that made it seem like a fair.

We heard the church tambourines from a block away.

"Sure wish we could get your father to come out to the Lord's house one of these mornings," said Mrs. Hunt. Then she looked at me. "What church do you usually go to, Tish?"

Well, as I've said, we were Baptists. But we didn't go to church very often—maybe Christmas or Easter, days like that. Mama didn't dig the church sisters, who didn't dig her, and Sis kind of takes after Mama, and Daddy didn't see any point in running after the Lord and he didn't seem to have very much respect for him.

I said, "We go to Abyssinia Baptist," and looked at the cracks in the sidewalk.

"That's a very handsome church," said Mrs. Hunt—as though that was the best thing that could possibly be said about it and that that certainly wasn't much.

It was eleven in the morning. Service had just begun. Actually, Sunday school had begun at nine and Fonny was usually supposed to be in church for that; but on this Sunday morning he had been given a special dispensation because of me. And the truth is, too, that Mrs. Hunt was kind of lazy and didn't really like getting up that early to make sure Fonny was in Sunday school. In Sunday school, there wasn't anybody to admire her—her carefully washed and covered body and her snow-white soul. Frank was not about to get up and take Fonny off to Sunday school and the sisters didn't want to dirty their hands on their nappy-headed brother. So, Mrs. Hunt, sighing deeply and praising the Lord, would have to get up and get Fonny dressed. But, of course, if she didn't take him to Sunday school by the hand, he didn't usually get there. And, many times, that woman fell out happy in church without knowing the whereabouts of her only son: "Whatever Alice don't feel like being bothered with," Frank was to say to me, much later, "she leaves in the hands of Lord."

The church had been a post office. I don't know how come the building had had to be sold, or why, come to that, anybody had wanted to buy it, because it still looked like a post office, long and dark and low. They had knocked down some walls and put in some benches and put up the church signs and the church schedules; but the ceiling was that awful kind of wrinkled tin, and they had either painted it brown or they had left it unpainted. When you came in, the pulpit looked a mighty long ways off. To tell the truth, I think the people in the church were just proud that their church was so big and that they had somehow got their hands on it. Of course I was (more or less) used to Abyssinia. It was brighter, and had a balcony. I used to sit in that balcony, on Mama's knees. Every time I think of a certain song, "Uncloudy Day," I'm back in that balcony again, on Mama's knees. Every time I hear "Blessed Quietness," I think of Fonny's church and Fonny's mother. I don't mean that either the song or the church was quiet. But I don't remember ever hearing that song in our church. I'll always associate that song with Fonny's church because when they sang it on that Sunday morning, Fonny's mother got happy.

Watching people get happy and fall out under the Power is always something to see, even if you see it all the time. But people didn't often get happy in our church: we were more respectable, more civilized, than sanctified. I still find something in it very frightening: but I think this is because Fonny hated it.

That church was so wide, it had three aisles. Now, just to the contrary of what you might think, it's much harder to find the central aisle than it is when there's just one aisle down the middle. You have to have an instinct for it. We entered that church and Mrs. Hunt led us straight down the aisle which was farthest to the left, so that everybody from two aisles over had to turn and watch us. And—frankly—we were something to watch. There was black, long-legged me, in a blue dress, with my hair straightened and with a blue ribbon in it. There was Fonny, who held me by the hand, in a kind of agony, in his white shirt, blue suit, and blue tie, his hair grimly, despairingly shining not so much from the Vaseline in his hair as from the sweat in his scalp; and there was Mrs. Hunt, who, somehow, I don't know how, from the moment we walked through the church doors, became filled with a stern love for her two little heathens and marched us before her to the mercy seat. She was wearing something pink or beige, I'm not quite sure now, but in all that gloom, it showed. And she was wearing one of those awful hats women used to wear which have a veil on them which stops at about the level of the eyebrow or the nose and which always makes you look like you have some disease. And she wore high heels, too, which made a certain sound, something like pistols, and she carried her head very high and noble. She was saved the moment she entered the church, she was Sanctified holy, and I even remember until today how much she made me tremble, all of a sudden, deep inside. It was like there was nothing, nothing, nothing you could ever hope to say to her unless you wanted to pass through the hands of the living God: and He would check it out with her before He answered you. The mercy seat: she led us to the front row and sat us down before it. She made us sit but she knelt, on her knees, I mean, in front of her seat, and bowed her head and covered her eyes, making sure she didn't fuck with that veil. I stole a look at Fonny, but Fonny wouldn't look at me. Mrs. Hunt rose, she faced the entire congregation for a moment and then she, modestly, sat down.

Somebody was testifying, a young man with kind of reddish hair, he was talking about the Lord and how the Lord had dyed all the spots out of his soul and taken all the lust out of his flesh. When I got older, I used to see him around. His name was George: I used to see him nodding on the stoop or on the curb, and he died of an overdose. The congregation amened him to death, a big sister, in the pulpit, in her long white robe, jumped up and did a little shout; they cried, Help him, Lord Jesus, help him! and the moment he sat down, another sister, her name was Rose and not much later she was going to disappear from the church and have a baby—and I still remember the last time I saw her, when I was about fourteen, walking the streets in the snow with her face all marked and her hands all swollen and a rag around her head and her stockings falling down, singing to herself—stood up and started singing, *How did you feel when you come out the wilderness, leaning on the Lord?*

Then Fonny did look at me, just for a second. Mrs. Hunt was singing and clapping her hands. And a kind of fire in the congregation mounted.

Now, I began to watch another sister, seated on the other side of Fonny, darker and plainer than Mrs. Hunt but just as well dressed, who was throwing up her hands and crying, Holy! Holy! Holy! Bless your name, Jesus! Bless your name, Jesus! And Mrs. Hunt started crying out and seemed to be answering her: it was like they were trying to outdo each other. And the sister was dressed in blue, dark, dark blue and she was wearing a matching blue hat, the kind of hat that sits back—like a skull cap—and the hat had a white rose in it and every time she moved it moved, every time she bowed the white rose bowed. The white rose was like some weird kind of light, especially since she was so dark and in such a dark dress. Fonny and I just sat there between them, while the voices of the congregation rose and rose and rose around us, without any mercy at all. Fonny and I weren't touching each other and we didn't look at each other and yet we were holding on to each other, like children in a rocking boat. A boy in the back, I got to know him later, too, his name was Teddy, a big brown-skinned boy, heavy everywhere except just where he should have been, thighs, hands, behind, and feet, something like a mushroom turned upside down, started singing, "Blessed quietness, holy quietness."

"What assurance in my soul," sang Mrs. Hunt.

"On the stormy sea," sang the dark sister, on the other side of Fonny.

"Jesus speaks to me," sang Mrs. Hunt.

"And the billows cease *to roll!"* sang the dark sister.

Teddy had the tambourine, and this gave the cue to the piano player—I never got to know him: a long dark, evil-looking brother, with hands made for strangling; and with these hands he attacked the keyboard like he was beating the brains out of someone he remembered. No doubt, the congregation had their memories, too, and they went to pieces. The church began to rock. And rocked me and Fonny, too, though they didn't know it, and in a very different way. Now, we knew that nobody loved us: or, now, we knew who did. Whoever loved us was not here.

It's funny what you hold on to to get through terror when terror surrounds you. I guess I'll remember until I die that black lady's white rose. Suddenly, it seemed to stand straight up, in that awful place, and I grabbed Fonny's hand—I didn't know I'd grabbed it; and, on either side of us, all of a sudden, the two women were dancing—shouting: the holy dance. The lady with the rose had her head forward and the rose moved like lightning around her head, our heads, and the lady with the veil had her head back: the veil which was now far above her forehead, which framed that forehead, seemed like the sprinkling of black water, baptizing us and sprinkling her. People moved around us, to give them room, and they danced into the middle aisle. Both of them held their handbags. Both of them wore high heels.

Fonny and I never went to church again. We have

never talked about our first date. Only, when I first had to go and see him in the Tombs, and walked up those steps and into those halls, it was just like walking into church.

Now that I had told Fonny about the baby, I knew I had to tell: Mama and Sis—but her real name is Ernestine, she's four years older than me—and Daddy and Frank. I got off the bus and I didn't know which way to go—a few blocks west, to Frank's house, or one block east, to mine. But I felt so funny, I thought I'd better get home. I really wanted to tell Frank before I told Mama. But I didn't think I could walk that far.

My Mama's a kind of strange woman—so people say —and she was twenty-four when I was born, so she's past forty now. I must tell you, I love her. I think she's a beautiful woman. She may not be beautiful to look at— whatever the fuck *that* means, in this kingdom of the blind. Mama's started to put on a little weight. Her hair is turning gray, but only way down on the nape of her neck, in what her generation called the "kitchen," and in the very center of her head—so she's gray, visibly, only if she bows her head or turns her back, and God knows she doesn't often do either. If she's facing you, she's black on black. Her name is Sharon. She used to try to be a singer, and she was born in Birmingham; she managed to get out of that corner of hell by the time she was nineteen, running away with a traveling band, but, more especially, with the drummer. That didn't work out, because, as she says,

"I don't know if I ever loved him, really. I was young but I think now that I was younger than I should have been, for my age. If you see what I mean. Anyway, I know I wasn't woman enough to help the man, to give him what he needed."

He went one way and she went another and she ended up in Albany, of all places, working as a barmaid. She was twenty and had come to realize that, though she had a voice, she wasn't a singer; that to endure and embrace the life of a singer demands a whole lot more than a voice. This meant that she was kind of lost. She felt herself going under; people were going under around her, every day; and Albany isn't exactly God's gift to black folks, either.

Of course, I must say that I don't think America is God's gift to anybody—if it is, God's days have *got* to be numbered. That God these people say they serve—and *do* serve, in ways that they don't know—has got a very nasty sense of humor. Like you'd beat the shit out of Him, if He was a man. Or: if *you* were.

In Albany, she met Joseph, my father, and she met him in the bus stop. She had just quit her job and he had just quit his. He's five years older than she is and he had been a porter in the bus station. He had come from Boston and he was really a merchant seaman; but he had sort of got himself trapped in Albany mainly because of this older woman he was going with then, who really just didn't dig him going on sea voyages. By the time Sharon, my mother, walked into that bus station with her little cardboard suitcase and her big scared eyes, things were just about ending between himself and this woman—Joseph didn't like bus stations—and it was the time of the Korean war, so he knew that if he didn't get back to sea soon, he'd be in the army and he certainly would not have dug *that*. As sometimes happens in life, everything came to a head at the same time: and here came Sharon.

He says, and I believe him, that he knew he wasn't going to let her out of his sight the moment he saw her walk away from the ticket window and sit down by herself on a bench and look around her. She was trying to look tough and careless, but she just looked scared. He says he wanted to laugh, and, at the same time, something in her frightened eyes made him want to cry.

He walked over to her, and he wasted no time.

"Excuse me, Miss. Are you going to the city?"

"To New York City, you mean?"

"Yes, Miss. To New York—city."

"Yes," she said, staring at him.

"I am too," he said, having just at that minute decided it, but being pretty sure that he had the money for a ticket on him, "but I don't know the city real well. Do you know it?"

"Why, no, not too well," she said, looking more scared than ever because she really didn't have any idea who this nut could be, or what he was after. She'd been to New York a few times, with her drummer.

"Well, I've got a uncle lives there," he said, "and he give me his address and I just wonder if you know where it is." He hardly knew New York at all, he'd always worked mainly out of San Francisco, and he gave Mama an address just off the top of his head, which made her look even more frightened. It was an address somewhere down off Wall Street.

"Why, yes," she said, "but I don't know if any colored people live down there." She didn't dare tell this maniac that *nobody* lived down there, there wasn't a damn thing down there but cafeterias, warehouses, and office buildings. "Only white people," she said, and she was kind of looking for a place to run.

"That's right," he said, "my uncle's a white man," and he sat down next to her.

He had to go to the ticket window to get his ticket, but he was afraid to walk away from her yet, he was afraid she'd disappear. And now the bus came, and she stood up. So he stood up and picked up her bag and said, "Allow me," and took her by the elbow and marched her over to the ticket window and she stood next to him while he bought his ticket. There really wasn't anything else that she could do, unless she wanted to start screaming for help; and she couldn't, anyway, stop him from getting on the bus. She hoped she'd figure out something before they got to New York.

Well, that was the last time my Daddy ever saw that bus station, and the very last time he carried a stranger's bags.

She hadn't got rid of him by the time they got to New York, of course; and he didn't seem to be in a great hurry to find his white uncle. They got to New York and he helped her get settled in a rooming house, and he went to the Y. And he came to get her the next morning, for breakfast. Within a week, he had married her and gone back to sea and my mother, a little stunned, settled down to live.

She'll take the news of the baby all right, I believe, and so will Sis Ernestine. Daddy may take it kind of rough but that's just because he doesn't know as much about his daughter as Mama and Ernestine do. Well. He'll be worried, too, in another way, and he'll show it more.

Nobody was home when I finally made it up to that top floor of ours. We've lived here for about five years, and it's not a bad apartment, as housing projects go. Fonny and I had been planning to fix up a loft down in the East Village, and we'd looked at quite a few. It just seemed better for us because we couldn't really afford to live in a project, and Fonny hates them and there'd be no place for Fonny to work on his sculpture. The other places in Harlem are even worse than the projects. You'd never be able to start your new life in those places, you remember them too well, and you'd never want to bring up your baby there. But it's something, when you think about it, how many babies *were* brought into those places, with rats as big as cats, roaches the size of mice, splinters the size of a man's finger, and somehow survived it. You don't want to think about those who didn't; and, to tell the truth, there's always something very sad in those who did, or do.

I hadn't been home more than five minutes when Mama walked through the door. She was carrying a shopping bag and she was wearing what I call her shopping hat, which is a kind of floppy beige beret.

"How you doing, Little One?" she smiled, but she gave me a sharp look, too. "How's Fonny?"

"He's just the same. He's fine. He sends his love."

"Good. You see the lawyer?"

"Not today. I have to go on Monday—you know—after work."

"He been to see Fonny?"

"No."

She sighed and took off her hat, and put it on the TV set. I picked up the shopping bag and we walked into the kitchen. Mama started putting things away.

I half sat, half leaned, on the sink, and I watched her. Then, for a minute there, I got scared and my belly kind of turned over. Then, I realized that I'm into my third month, I've *got* to tell. Nothing shows yet, but one day Mama's going to give me another sharp look.

And then, suddenly, half leaning, half sitting there, watching her—she was at the refrigerator, she looked critically at a chicken and put it away, she was kind of humming under her breath, but the way you hum when your mind is concentrated on something, something painful, just about to come around the corner, just about to hit you—I suddenly had this feeling that she already knew, had known all along, had only been waiting for me to tell her.

I said, "Mama—?"

"Yeah, Little Bit?" Still humming.

But I didn't say anything. So, after a minute, she closed the refrigerator door and turned and looked at me.

I started to cry. It was her look.

She stood there for a minute. She came and put a hand on my forehead and then a hand on my shoulder. She said, "Come on in my room. Your Daddy and Sis be here soon."

We went into her room and sat down on the bed and Mama closed the door. She didn't touch me. She just sat very still. It was like she had to be very together because I had gone to pieces.

She said, "Tish, I declare. I don't think you got nothing to cry about." She moved a little. "You tell Fonny?"

"I just told him today. I figured I should tell him first."

"You did right. And I bet he just grinned all over his face, didn't he?"

I kind of stole a look at her and I laughed, "Yes. He sure did."

"You must—let's see—you about three months gone?"

"Almost."

"What you crying about?"

Then she did touch me, she took me in her arms and she rocked me and I cried.

She got me a handkerchief and I blew my nose. She walked to the window and she blew hers.

"Now, listen," she said, "you got enough on your mind without worrying about being a bad girl and all that jive-ass shit. I sure hope I raised you better than that. If you was a bad girl, you wouldn't be sitting on that bed, you'd long been turning tricks for the warden."

She came back to the bed and sat down. She seemed to be raking her mind for the right words.

"Tish," she said, "when we was first brought here, the white man he didn't give us no preachers to say words over us before we had our babies. And you and Fonny be together right now, married or not, wasn't for that same damn white man. So, let me tell you what you got to do. You got to think about that baby. You got to hold on to that baby, don't care what else happens or don't happen. *You* got to do that. Can't nobody else do that for you. And the rest of us, well, we going to hold on to you. And we going to get Fonny out. Don't you worry. I know it's hard—but don't you worry. And that baby be the best thing that ever happened to Fonny. He needs that baby. It going to give him a whole lot of courage."

She put one finger under my chin, a trick she has sometimes, and looked me in the eyes, smiling.

"Am I getting through to you, Tish?"

"Yes, Mama. Yes."

"Now, when your Daddy and Ernestine get home, we going to sit at the table together, and *I'll* make the family announcement. I think that might be easier, don't you?"

"Yes. Yes."

She got up from the bed.

"Take off them streets clothes and lie down for a minute. I'll come get you."

She opened the door.

"Yes, Mama—Mama?"

"Yes, Tish?"

"Thank you, Mama."

She laughed. "Well, Tish, daughter, I do not know what you thanking me for, but you surely more than welcome."

She closed the door and I heard her in the kitchen. I took off my coat and my shoes and lay back on the bed. It was the hour when darkness begins, when the sounds of the night begin.

The doorbell rang. I heard Mama yell, "Be right there!" and then she came into the room again. She was carrying a small water glass with a little whiskey in it.

"Here. Sit up. Drink this. Do you good."

Then she closed the bedroom door behind her and I heard her heels along the hall that leads to the front door. It was Daddy, he was in a good mood, I heard his laugh.

"Tish home yet?"

"She's taking a little nap inside. She was kind of beat."

"She see Fonny?"

"Yeah. She saw Fonny. She saw the inside of the Tombs, too. That's why I made her lie down."

"What about the lawyer?"

"She going to see him Monday."

Daddy made a sound, I heard the refrigerator door open and close, and he poured himself a beer.

"Where's Sis?"

"She'll be here. She had to work late."

"How much you think them damn lawyers is going to cost us, before this thing is over?"

"Joe, you know damn well ain't no point in asking me that question."

"Well. They sure got it made, the rotten mother-fuckers."

"Amen to that."

By now, Mama had poured herself some gin and orange juice and was sitting at the table, opposite him. She was swinging her foot; she was thinking ahead.

"How'd it go today?"

"All right."

Daddy works on the docks. He doesn't go to sea anymore. *All right* means that he probably didn't have to curse out more than one or two people all day long, or threaten anybody with death.

Fonny gave Mama one of his first pieces of sculpture. This was almost two years ago. Something about it always makes me think of Daddy. Mama put it by itself on a small table in the living room. It's not very high, it's done in black wood. It's of a naked man with one hand at his forehead and the other half hiding his sex. The legs are long, very long, and very wide apart, and one foot seems planted, unable to move, and the whole motion of the figure is torment. It seemed a very strange figure for such a young kid to do, or, at least, it seemed strange until you thought about it. Fonny used to go to a vocational school where they teach kids to make all kinds of shitty, really useless things, like card tables and has-socks and chests of drawers which nobody's ever going to buy because who buys handmade furniture? The rich don't do it. They say the kids are dumb and so they're teaching them to work with their hands. Those kids aren't dumb. But the people who run these schools want to make sure that they don't get smart: they are really teaching the kids to be slaves. Fonny didn't go for it at all, and he split, taking most of the wood from the workshop with him. It took him about a week, tools one day, wood the next; but the wood was a problem because you can't put it in your pocket or under your coat; finally, he and a friend broke in the school after dark, damn near emptied the woodwork shop, and loaded the wood into the friend's brother's car. They hid some of the wood in the basement of a friendly janitor, and Fonny brought the tools to my house, and some of that wood is still under my bed.

Fonny had found something that he could do, that he wanted to do, and this saved him from the death that was waiting to overtake the children of our age. Though the death took many forms, though people died early in many different ways, the death itself was very simple and the cause was simple, too: as simple as a plague: the kids had been told that they weren't worth shit and everything they saw around them proved it. They struggled, they struggled, but they fell, like flies, and they congregated on the garbage heaps of their lives, like flies. And perhaps I clung to Fonny, perhaps Fonny saved *me* because he was just about the only boy I knew who wasn't fooling around with the needles or drinking cheap wine or mugging people or holding up stores—

and he never got his hair conked: it just stayed nappy. He started working as a short-order cook in a barbecue joint, so he could eat, and he found a basement where he could work on his wood and he was at our house more often than he was at his own house.

At his house, there was always fighting. Mrs. Hunt couldn't stand Fonny, or Fonny's ways, and the two sisters sided with Mrs. Hunt—especially because, now, they were in terrible trouble. They had been raised to be married but there wasn't anybody around them good enough for them. They were really just ordinary Harlem girls, even though they'd made it as far as City College. But absolutely nothing was happening for them at City College—nothing: the brothers with degrees didn't want them; those who wanted their women black wanted them black; and those who wanted their women white wanted them white. So, there they were, and they blamed it all on Fonny. Between the mother's prayers, which were more like curses, and the sisters' tears, which were more like orgasms, Fonny didn't stand a chance. Neither was Frank a match for these three hags. He just got angry, and you can just about imagine the shouting that went on in that house. And Frank had started drinking. I couldn't blame him. And sometimes he came to our house, too, pretending that he was looking for Fonny. It was much worse for him than it was for Fonny; and he had lost the tailor shop and was working in the garment center. He had started to depend on Fonny now, the way Fonny had once depended on him. Neither of them, anyway, as you can see, had any other house they could go to. Frank went to bars, but Fonny didn't like bars.

That same passion which saved Fonny got him into trouble, and put him in jail. For, you see, he had found his center, his own center, inside him: and it showed. He wasn't anybody's nigger. And that's a crime, in this fucking free country. You're suppose to be *somebody's* nigger. And if you're nobody's nigger, you're a bad nigger: and that's what the cops decided when Fonny moved downtown.

Ernestine has come in, with her bony self. I can hear her teasing Daddy.

She works with kids in a settlement house way downtown—kids up to the age of fourteen or so, all colors, boys and girls. It's very hard work, but she digs it—I guess if she didn't dig it, she couldn't do it. It's funny about people. When Ernestine was little she was as vain as vain could be. She always had her hair curled and her dresses were always clean and she was always in front of that damn mirror, like she just could not believe how beautiful she was. I hated her. Since she was nearly four years older than me, she considered me beneath her notice. We fought like cats and dogs, or maybe it was more like two bitches.

Mama tried not to worry too much about it. She figured that Sis—I called her Sis as a way of calling her out of her name and also, maybe, as a way of claiming her—was probably cut out for show business, and would end up on the stage. This thought did not fill her heart with joy: but she had to remember, my mother, Sharon, that she had once tried to be a singer.

All of a sudden, it almost seemed like from one day to the next, all that changed. Sis got tall, for one thing, tall and skinny. She took to wearing slacks and tying up her hair and she started reading books like books were going out of style. Whenever I'd come home from school and she was there, she'd be curled up on something, or lying on the floor, reading. She stopped reading newspapers. She stopped going to the movies. "I don't need no more of the white man's lying shit," she said. "He's fucked with my mind enough already." At the same time, she didn't become rigid or unpleasant and she didn't talk, not for a long time anyway, about what she read. She got to be much nicer to me. And her face began to change. It became bonier and more private, much more beautiful. Her long narrow eyes darkened with whatever it was they were beginning to see.

She gave up her plans for going to college, and worked for a while in a hospital. She met a little girl in that hospital, the little girl was dying, and, at the age of twelve, she was already a junkie. And this wasn't a black girl. She was Puerto Rican. And then Ernestine started working with children.

"Where's Jezebel?"

Sis started calling me Jezebel after I got my job at the perfume center of the department store where I work now. The store thought that it was very daring, very progressive, to give this job to a colored girl. I stand behind that damn counter all day long, smiling till my back teeth ache, letting tired old ladies smell the back of my hand. Sis claimed that I came home smelling like a Louisiana whore.

"She's home. She's lying down."

"She all right?"

"She's tired. She went to see Fonny."

"How's Fonny taking it?"

"Taking it."

"Lord. Let me make myself a drink. You want me to cook?"

"No. I'll get into the pots in a minute."

"She see Mr. Hayward?"

Arnold Hayward is the lawyer. Sis found him for me through the settlement house, which has been forced, after all, to have some dealings with lawyers.

"No. She's seeing him on Monday, after work."

"You going with her?"

"I think I better."

"Yeah. I think so, too—Daddy, you better stop putting down that beer, you getting to be as big as a house.—And I'll call him from work, before you all get there.—You want a shot of gin in that beer, old man?"

"Just put it on the side, daughter dear, before I stand up."

"Stand up!—Here!"

"And tan your hide. You better listen to Aretha when she sings 'Respect.'—You know, Tish says she thinks that lawyer wants more money."

"Daddy, we paid him his retainer, that's why ain't none of us got no clothes. And I know we got to pay expenses. But he ain't supposed to get no more *money* until he brings Fonny to trial."

"He says it's a tough case."

"Shit. What's a lawyer for?"

"To make money," Mama said.

"Well. Anybody talk to the Hunts lately?"

"They don't want to know nothing about it, you know that. Mrs. Hunt and them two camellias is just in disgrace. And poor Frank ain't got no money."

"Well. Let's not talk too much about it in front of Tish. We'll work it out somehow."

"Shit. We got to work it out. Fonny's like one of us."

"He *is* one of us," said Mama.

I turned on the lights in Mama's bedroom, so they'd know I was up, and I looked at myself in the mirror. I kind of patted my hair and I walked into the kitchen.

"Well," said Sis, "although I cannot say that your beauty rest did you a hell of a lot of good, I *do* admire the way you persevere."

Mama said that if we wanted to eat, we'd better get our behinds out of her kitchen, and so we went into the living room.

I sat on the hassock, leaning on Daddy's knee. Now, it was seven o'clock and the streets were full of noises. I felt very quiet after my long day, and my baby began to be real to me. I don't mean that it hadn't been real before; but, now, in a way, I was alone with it. Sis had left the lights very low. She put on a Ray Charles record and sat down on the sofa.

I listened to the music and the sounds from the streets

and Daddy's hand rested lightly on my hair. And everything seemed connected—the street sounds, and Ray's voice and his piano and my Daddy's hand and my sister's silhouette and the sounds and the lights coming from the kitchen. It was as though we were a picture, trapped in time: this had been happening for hundreds of years, people sitting in a room, waiting for dinner, and listening to the blues. And it was as though, out of these elements, this patience, my Daddy's touch, the sounds of my mother in the kitchen, the way the light fell, the way the music continued beneath everything, the movement of Ernestine's head as she lit a cigarette, the movement of her hand as she dropped the match into the ashtray, the blurred human voices rising from the street, out of this rage and a steady, somehow triumphant sorrow, my baby was slowly being formed. I wondered if it would have Fonny's eyes. As someone had wondered, not, after all, so very long ago, about the eyes of Joseph, my father, whose hand rested on my head. What struck me suddenly, more than anything else, was something I knew but hadn't looked at: this was Fonny's baby and mine, we had made it together, it was both of us. I didn't know either of us very well. What would both of us be like? But this, somehow, made me think of Fonny and made me smile. My father rubbed his hand over my forehead. I thought of Fonny's touch, of Fonny, in my arms, his breath, his touch, his odor, his weight, that terrible and beautiful presence riding into me and his breath being snarled, as if by a golden thread, deeper and deeper in his throat as he rode—as he rode deeper and deeper not so much into me as into a kingdom which lay just behind his eyes. He worked on wood that way. He worked on stone that way. If I had never seen him work, I might never have known he loved me.

It's a miracle to realize that somebody loves you.

"Tish?"

Ernestine, gesturing with her cigarette.

"Yes."

"What time you seeing the lawyer on Monday?"

"After the six o'clock visit. I'll be there about seven. He says he's got to work late, anyway."

"If he says anything about more money, you tell him to call me, you hear?"

"I don't know what good that's going to do, if he wants more money, he wants more money——"

"You do like your sister tells you," Daddy said.

"He won't talk to you," Ernestine said, "the way he'll talk to me, can you dig it?"

"Yes," I said, finally, "I can dig it." But, for reasons I couldn't explain, something in her voice frightened me to death. I felt the way I'd felt all day, alone with my trouble. Nobody could help me, not even Sis. Because she was certainly determined to help me, I knew that. But maybe I realized that she was frightened, too, although she was trying to sound calm and tough. I realized that she knew a whole lot about it because of the kids downtown. I wanted to ask her how it worked. I wanted to ask her *if* it worked.

When there's nobody but us we eat in the kitchen, which is maybe the most important room in our house, the room where everything happens, where things begin and take their shape and end. Now, when supper was over that night, Mama went to the cupboard and came back with an old bottle, a bottle she's had for years, of very old French brandy. They came from her days as a singer, her days with the drummer. This was the last bottle, it hadn't been opened yet. She put the bottle on the table, in front of Joseph, and she said, "Open it." She got four glasses and then she stood there while he opened it. Ernestine and Joseph looked like they just couldn't guess what had got into Mama: but I knew what she was doing, and my heart jumped up.

Daddy got the bottle open. Mama said, "You the man of the house, Joe. Start pouring."

It's funny about people. Just before something happens, you almost know what it is. You *do* know what it is, I believe. You just haven't had the time—and now you *won't* have the time—to say it to yourself. Daddy's face changed in a way I can't describe. His face became as definite as stone, every line and angle suddenly seemed chiseled, and his eyes turned a blacker black. He was waiting—suddenly, helplessly—for what was already known to be translated, to enter reality, to be born.

Sis watched Mama with her eyes very calm, her eyes very long and narrow, smiling a little.

No one looked at me. I was there, then, for them, in a way that had nothing to do with me. I was there, then, for them, like Fonny was present, like my baby, just beginning now, out of a long, long sleep, to turn, to listen, to awaken, somewhere beneath my heart.

Daddy poured and Mama gave us each a glass. She looked at Joseph, then at Ernestine, then at me—she smiled at me.

"This is sacrament," she said, "and, no, I ain't gone crazy. We're drinking to a new life. Tish is going to have Fonny's baby." She touched Joseph. "Drink," she said.

Daddy wet his lips, staring at me. It was like no one could speak before he spoke. I stared at him. I didn't know what he was going to say. Joseph put his glass down. Then he picked it up again. He was trying to speak; he wanted to speak; but he couldn't. And he looked at me as if he was trying to find out something, something my face would tell him. A strange smile wavered just around his face, not yet *in* his face, and he seemed to be traveling backward and forward at once, in time. He said, "That's a hell of a note." Then he drank some more brandy, and he said, "Ain't you going to drink to the little one, Tish?" I swallowed a little brandy, and I coughed and Ernestine patted me on the back. Then, she took me in her arms. She had tears on her face. She smiled down at me—but she didn't say anything.

"How long this been going on?" Daddy asked.

"About three months," Mama said.

"Yeah. That's what I figured," said Ernestine, surprising me.

"Three months!" Daddy said: as though five months or two months would have made some kind of difference and made more sense.

"Since March," I said. Fonny had been arrested in March.

"While you two was running around looking at places, so you could get married," Daddy said. His face was full of questions, and he would have been able to ask these questions of his son—or, at least, I think that a black man can: but he couldn't ask these questions of his daughter. For a moment, I was almost angry, then I wasn't. Fathers and sons are one thing. Fathers and daughters are another.

It doesn't do to look too hard into this mystery, which is as far from being simple as it is from being safe. We don't know enough about ourselves. I think it's better to know that you don't know, that way you can grow with the mystery as the mystery grows in you. But, these days, of course, everybody knows everything, that's why so many people are so lost.

But I wondered how Frank would take the news that his son, Fonny, was about to be a father. Then I realized that the first thing everybody thought was, *But Fonny's in jail!* Frank would think that: that would be his first thought. Frank would think, if anything happens, my boy won't never see his baby. And Joseph thought, If anything happens, my little girl's baby won't have no father. Yes. That was the thought, unspoken, which stiffened the air in our kitchen. And I felt that I should say something. But I was too tired. I leaned against Ernestine's shoulder. I had nothing to say.

"You sure you want this baby, Tish?" my father asked me.

"Oh, yes," I said, "and Fonny wants it, too! It's *our baby*," I said. "Don't you see? And it's not Fonny's fault that he is in jail, it's not as though he ran away, or anything. And—" this was the only way I could answer the questions he hadn't asked—"we've always been best friends, ever since we were little, you know that. And we'd be married now, if—if—!"

"Your father know that," Mama said. "He's only worried about you."

"Don't you go thinking I think you a bad girl, or any foolishness like that," Daddy said. "I just asked you that because you so young, that's all, and——"

"It's rough, but we'll make it," Ernestine said.

She knows Daddy better than I do. I think it's because she's felt since we were children that our Daddy maybe loved me more than he loves her. This isn't true, and she knows that now—people love different people in different ways—but it must have seemed that way to her when we were little. I look as though I just can't make it, she looks like can't nothing stop her. If you look helpless, people react to you in one way and if you look strong, or just come on strong, people react to you in another way, and, since you don't see what they see, this can be very painful. I think that's maybe why Sis was always in front of that damn mirror all the time, when we were kids. She was saying, *I don't care. I got me.* Of course, this only made her come on stronger than ever, which was the last effect she desired: but that's the way we are and that's how we can sometimes get so fucked up. Anyway, she's past all that. She knows who she is, or, at least, she knows who she damn well isn't; and since she's no longer terrified of uprisings in those forces which she lives with and has learned how to use and subdue, she can walk straight ahead into anything; and so she can cut Daddy off when he's talking —which I can't do. She moved away from me a little and put my glass in my hand. "Unbow your head, sister," she said, and raised her glass and touched mine. "Save the children," she said, very quietly, and drained her glass.

Mama said, "To the newborn," and Daddy said, "I hope it's a boy. That'd tickle old Frank to pieces, I bet." Then he looked at me. "Do you mind," he asked me, "if I'm the one to tell him, Tish?"

I said, "No. I don't mind."

"Well, then!" he said, grinning, "maybe I'll go on over there now."

"Maybe you better phone first," Mama said. "He don't stay home a whole lot, you know."

"I sure would like to be the one to tell them sisters," said Ernestine.

Mama laughed, and said, "Joe, why don't you just call up and ask them all over here? Hell, it's Saturday night and it ain't late and we still got a lot of brandy in the bottle. And, now that I think about it, it's really the best way to do it."

"That's all right with you, Tish?" Daddy asked me.

"It's got to be done," I said.

So, Daddy stood up, after watching me for a moment, and walked into the living room, to the phone. He could have used the wall phone in the kitchen but he had that kind of grim smile on his face which he has when he knows he's got business to take care of and when he wants to make sure you know enough to stay out of it.

We listened to him dialing the number. That was the only sound in the house. Then, we could hear the phone at the other end, ringing. Daddy cleared his throat.

We heard, "Mrs. Hunt—? Oh. Good evening, Mrs. Hunt. This is Joe Rivers talking. I just wondered if I could please speak to Frank, if he's home—Thank you, Mrs. Hunt."

Mama grunted, and winked at Sis.

"Hey!—How you doing? Yeah, this is Joe. I'm all right, man, hanging in, you know—say, listen—oh, yeah, Tish saw him this afternoon, man, he's fine.—Yeah—As a matter of *fact*, man, we got a whole *lot* to talk about, that's why I'm calling you.—I can't go into all that over the phone, man. Listen. It concerns all of us—Yes.—Listen. Don't give me all that noise. You all just jump in the car and come on over here. Now. Yeah. That's right. *Now*—What?—Look, man, I said it concerns *all* of us. —Ain't nobody here dressed neither, she can come in her fucking *bathrobe* for all I care.—Shut up, you sick mother. I'm trying to be nice. Shit. Don't be bitter—Just dump her in the back seat of the *car*, and *drive*, now, come on, man. This is *serious*.—Hey. Pick up a six pack, I'll pay you when you get here.—Yeah.—Look. Will you hang up this phone and get your ass, I mean your *collective* ass, on over here, man?—In a minute. Bye."

He came back into the kitchen, smiling.

"Mrs. Hunt is getting dressed," he said, and sat down. Then he looked over at me. He smiled—a wonderful smile. "Come on over here, Tish," he said, "and sit down on your Daddy's knee."

I felt like a princess. I swear I did. He took me in his arms and settled me on his lap and kissed me on the forehead and rubbed his hand, at first roughly and then very gently through my hair. "You're a good girl, Clementine," he said. "I'm proud of you. Don't you forget that."

"She ain't going to forget it," said Ernestine. "I'll whip her ass."

"But she's *pregnant!*" Mama cried, and took a sip of her cognac and then we all cracked up. My father's chest shook with laughter, I felt his chest rising and falling between my shoulder blades, and this laughter contained a furious joy, an unspeakable relief: in spite of all that hung above our heads. I was his daughter, all right: I had found someone to love and I was loved and he was released and verified. That child in my belly was also, after all, *his* child, too, for there would have been no Tish if there had been no Joseph. Our laughter in that kitchen, then, was our helpless response to a miracle. That baby was our baby, it was on its way, my father's great hand on my belly held it and warmed it: in spite of all that hung above our heads, that child was promised safety. Love had sent it, spinning out of us, to us. Where that might take us, no one knew: but, now, my father, Joe, was ready. In a deadlier and more profound way than his daughters were, this child was the seed of his loins. And no knife could cut him off from life until that child was born. And I almost felt the child feel this, that child which had no movement yet—I almost felt it leap against my father's hand, kicking upward against my ribs. Something in me sang and hummed and then I felt the deadly morning sickness and I dropped my head onto my father's shoulder. He held me. It was very silent. The nausea passed.

Sharon watched it all, smiling, swinging her foot, thinking ahead. Again, she winked at Ernestine.

"Shall we," asked Ernestine, rising, "dress for Mrs. Hunt?"—and we all cracked up again.

"Look. We got to be nice," said Joseph.

"We'll be nice," said Ernestine. "Lord knows we'll be nice. You *raised* us right. You just didn't never buy us no *clothes*." She said to Mama, "But Mrs. Hunt, now, and them sisters, they got *wardrobes*—! Ain't no sense in trying to compete with them," she said despairingly, and sat down.

"I didn't run no tailor shop," said Joseph, and looked into my eyes, and smiled.

The very first time Fonny and I made love was strange. It was strange because we had both seen it coming. That is not exactly the way to put it. We had *not* seen it coming. Abruptly, it was there: and then we knew that it had always been there, waiting. We had not seen the moment. But the moment had seen us, from a long ways off—sat there, waiting for us—utterly free, the moment, playing cards, hurling thunderbolts, cracking spines, tremendously waiting for us, dawdling home from school, to keep our appointment.

Look. I dumped water over Fonny's head and scrubbed Fonny's back in the bathtub, in a time that seems a long time ago now. I swear I don't remember seeing his sex, and yet, of course, I must have. We never played doctor—and yet, I had played this rather terrifying game with other boys and Fonny had certainly played with other girls, and boys. I don't remember that we ever had any curiosity concerning each other's bodies at all —due to the cunning of that watching moment which knew we were approaching. Fonny loved me too much, we needed each other too much. We were a part of each other, flesh of each other's flesh—which meant that we so took each other for granted that we never thought of the flesh. He had legs, and I had legs—that wasn't all we knew but that was all we used. They brought us up the stairs and down the stairs and, always, to each other.

But that meant that there had never been any occasion for shame between us. I was flatchested for a very long time. I'm only beginning to have real breasts now, because of the baby, in fact, and I still don't have any hips. Fonny liked me so much that it didn't occur to him that he loved me. I liked him so much that no other boy was real to me. I didn't see them. I didn't know what this meant. But the waiting moment, which had spied us on the road, and which was waiting for us, knew.

Fonny kissed me good-night one night when he was twenty-one and I eighteen, and I felt his sex jerk against me and he moved away. I said good-night and I ran up the stairs and he ran down the stairs. And I couldn't sleep that night: something had happened. And he didn't come around, I didn't see him, for two or three weeks. That was when he did that wood figure which he gave to Mama.

The day he gave it to her was a Saturday. After he gave the figure to Mama we left the house and we walked around. I was so happy to see him, after so long, that I was ready to cry. And everything was different. I was walking through streets I had never seen before. The faces around me, I had never seen. We moved in a silence which was music from everywhere. Perhaps for the first time in my life, I was happy and knew that I was happy, and Fonny held me by the hand. It was like that Sunday morning, so long ago, when his mother had carried us to church.

Fonny had no part in his hair now—it was heavy all over his head. He had no blue suit, he had no suit at all. He was wearing an old black and red lumber jacket and old gray corduroy pants. His heavy shoes were scuffed; and he smelled of fatigue.

He was the most beautiful person I had seen in all my life.

He has a slow, long-legged, bowlegged walk. We walked down the stairs to the subway train, he holding me by the hand. The train, when it came, was crowded, and he put an arm around me for protection. I suddenly looked up into his face. No one can describe this, I really shouldn't try. His face was bigger than the world, his eyes deeper than the sun, more vast than the desert, all that had ever happened since time began was in his face. He smiled: a little smile. I saw his teeth: I saw exactly where the missing tooth had been, that day he spat in my mouth. The train rocked, he held me closer, and a kind of sigh I'd never heard before stifled itself in him.

It's astounding the first time you realize that a stranger has a body—the realization that he has a body makes him a stranger. It means that you have a body, too. You will live with this forever, and it will spell out the language of your life.

And it was absolutely astonishing to me to realize that I was a virgin. I really was. I suddenly wondered how. I wondered why. But it was because I had always, without ever thinking about it, known that I would spend my life with Fonny. It simply had not entered my mind that my life could do anything else. This meant that I was not merely a virgin; I was still a child.

We got off the train at Sheridan Square, in the Village. We walked east along West Fourth Street. Since it was Saturday, the streets were crowded, unbalanced with the weight of people. Most of them were young, they had to be young, you could see that: but they didn't seem young to me. They frightened me, I could not, then, have said why. I thought it was because they knew so much more than me. And they did. But, in another way, which I'm only beginning to understand now, they didn't. They had it all together: the walk, the sound, the laughter, the untidy clothes—clothes which were copies of a poverty as unimaginable for them as theirs was inexpressibly remote from me. There were many blacks and whites together: it was hard to tell which was the imitation. They were so free that they believed in nothing; and didn't realize that this illusion was their only truth and that they were doing exactly as they had been told.

Fonny looked over at me. It was getting to be between six and seven.

"You all right?"

"Sure. You?"

"You want to eat down here or you want to wait till we get back uptown or you want to go to the movies or you want a little wine or a little pot or a beer or a cup of coffee? Or you just want to walk a little more before you make up your mind?" He was grinning, warm and sweet, and pulling a little against my hand, and swinging it.

I was very happy, but I was uncomfortable, too. I had never been uncomfortable with him before.

"Let's walk to the park first." I somehow wanted to stay outside awhile.

"Okay." And he still had that funny smile on his face, like something wonderful had just happened to him and no one in the world knew anything about it yet, but him. But he would tell somebody soon, and it would be me.

We crossed crowded Sixth Avenue, all kinds of people out hunting for Saturday night. But nobody looked at us, because we were together and we were both black. Later, when I had to walk these streets alone, it was different, the people were different, and I was certainly no longer a child.

"Let's go this way," he said, and we started down Sixth Avenue, toward Bleecker Street. We started down Bleecker and Fonny stared for a moment through the big window of the San Remo. There was no one in there that he knew, and the whole place looked tired and discouraged, as though wearily about to shave and get dressed for a terrible evening. The people under the weary light were veterans of indescribable wars. We kept walking. The streets were very crowded now, with youngsters, black and white, and cops. Fonny held his head a little higher, and his grip tightened on my hand. There were lots of kids on the sidewalk, before the crowded coffee shop. A jukebox was playing Aretha's "That's Life." It was strange. Everyone was in the streets, moving and talking, like people do everywhere, and yet none of it seemed to be friendly. There was something hard and frightening about it: the way that something which looks real, but isn't, can send you screaming out of your mind. It was just like scenes uptown, in a way, with the older men and women sitting on the stoops; with small children running up and down the block, cars moving slowly through this maelstrom, the cop car parked on the corner, with the two cops in it, other cops swaggering slowly along the sidewalk. It was like scenes uptown, in a way, but with something left out, or something put in, I couldn't tell: but it was a scene that frightened me. One had to make one's way carefully here, for all these people were blind.

We were jostled, and Fonny put his arm around my shoulder. We passed Minetta Tavern, crossed Minetta Lane, passed the newspaper stand on the next corner, and crossed diagonally into the park, which seemed to huddle in the shadow of the heavy new buildings of NYU and the high new apartment buildings on the east and the north. We passed the men who had been playing chess in the lamplight for generations, and people walking their dogs, and young men with bright hair and very tight pants, who looked quickly at Fonny and resignedly at me. We sat down on the stone edge of the dry fountain, facing the arch. There were lots of people around us, but I still felt this terrible lack of friendliness.

"I've slept in this park sometimes," said Fonny. "It's not a good idea." He lit a cigarette. "You want a cigarette?"

"Not now." I had wanted to stay outside for a while. But now I wanted to get in, away from these people, out of the park. "Why did you sleep in the park?"

"It was late. I didn't want to wake up my folks. And I didn't have no bread."

"You could have come to *our* house."

"Well. I didn't want to wake up none of *you* neither." He put his cigarettes back into his pocket. "But I got me a pad down here now. I'll show it to you later, you want to see it." He looked at me. "You getting cold and tired, I'll get you something to eat, okay?"

"Okay. You got money?"

"Yeah, I hustled me up a little change, baby. Come on."

We did a lot of walking that night, because now Fonny took me way west, along Greenwich, past the Women's House of Detention, to this little Spanish restaurant, where Fonny knew all the waiters and they all knew him. And these people were different from the people in the street, their smiles were different, and I felt at home. It was Saturday, but it was early, and they put us at a small table in the back—not as though they didn't want people to see us but as though they were glad we'd come and wanted us to stay as long as possible.

I hadn't had much experience in restaurants, but Fonny had; he spoke a little Spanish, too, and I could see that the waiters were teasing him about me. And then I remembered, as I was being introduced to our waiter, Pedrocito—which meant that he was the youngest—that we had been called on the block, Romeo and Juliet, people had always teased us. But not like this.

Some days, days I took off, when I could see him in the middle of the day, and then, again, at six, I'd walk from Centre Street to Greenwich, and I'd sit in the back and they'd feed me, very silently and carefully making sure that I ate—something; more than once, Luisito, who had just arrived from Spain and who could barely speak English, took away the cold omelette which he had cooked and which I had not touched and brought me a new, hot one, saying, "Señorita—? *Por favor*. He and the *muchacho* need your strength. He will not forgive us, if we let you starve. We are his friends. He trusts us. You must trust us, too." He would pour me a little red wine. "Wine is good. *Slow*–ly." I would take a sip. He would smile, but he would not move until I began to eat. Then, "It will be a boy," he said, and grinned and moved away. They got me through many and many a terrible day. They were the very nicest people I had met in all New York; they cared. When the going got rough, when I was heavy, with Joseph, and Frank, and Sharon working, and Ernestine in battle, they would arrange to have errands in the neighborhood of the Tombs, and, as though it were the most natural thing in the world—which it was, for them—drive me to their restaurant, and then they would drive me back down for the six o'clock visit. I will never forget them, never: they knew.

But on this particular Saturday night, we did not know; Fonny did not know, and we were happy, all of us. I had one margherita, though we all knew that this was against the goddam motherfucking shit-eating *law*, and Fonny had a whiskey because at twenty-one you have a legal right to drink. His hands are big. He took my hands and put his hands in mine. "I want to show you something later," he said. I could not tell whose hands were trembling, which hands were holding. "Okay," I said. He had ordered paella and when it came we unjoined our hands and Fonny, elaborately, served me. "Next time it's your turn," he said, and we laughed and began to eat. And we had wine. And there were candles. And other people came, looking at us strangely, but, "We know the cats who own the joint," Fonny said, and we laughed again, and we were safe.

I had never seen Fonny outside of the world in which I moved. I had seen him with his father and his mother and his sisters, and I had seen him with us. But I'm not sure, now that I think about it, that I had ever really seen him with *me*: not until this moment when we were leaving the restaurant and all the waiters were laughing and talking with him, in Spanish and in English, and Fonny's face opened in a way I'd never seen it open and that laugh of his came rumbling up from his balls, from *their* balls—I had certainly never seen him, anyway, in the world in which *he* moved. Perhaps it was only now that I saw him with me, for he was turned away from me, laughing, but he was holding on to my hand. He was a stranger to me, but joined. I had never seen him with other men. I had never seen the love and respect that men can have for each other.

I've had time since to think about it. I think that the first time a woman sees this—though I was not yet a woman—she sees it, first of all, only because she loves the man: she could not possibly see it otherwise. It can be a very great revelation. And, in this fucked up time and place, many women, perhaps most women, feel, in this warmth and energy, a threat. They think that they feel locked out. The truth is that they sense themselves in the presence, so to speak, of a language which they cannot decipher and therefore cannot manipulate, and, however they make a thing about it, so far from being locked out, are appalled by the apprehension that they are, in fact, forever locked in. Only a man can see in the face of a woman the girl she was. It is a secret which can be revealed only to a particular man, and, then, only at his insistence. But men have no secrets, except from women, and never grow up in the way that women do. It is very much harder, and it takes much longer, for a man to grow up, and he could never do it at all without women. This is a mystery which can terrify and immobilize a woman, and it is always the key to her deepest distress. She must watch and guide, but he must lead, and he will always appear to be giving far more of his real attention to his comrades than he is giving to her. But that noisy, outward openness of men with each other enables them to deal with the silence and secrecy of women, that silence and secrecy which contains the truth of a man, and releases it. I suppose that the root of the resentment—a resentment which hides a bottomless terror—has to do with the fact that a woman is tremendously controlled by what the man's imagination makes of her—literally, hour by hour, day by day; so she becomes a woman. But a man exists in his own imagination, and can never be at the mercy of a woman's. —Anyway, in this fucked up time and place, the whole thing becomes ridiculous when you realize that women are supposed to be more imaginative than men. This is an idea dreamed up by men, and it proves exactly the contrary. The truth is that dealing with the reality of men leaves a woman very little time, or need, for imagination. And you can get very fucked up, here, once you take seriously the notion that a man who is not afraid to trust his imagination (which is all that men have ever trusted) is effeminate. It says a lot about this country, because, of course, if all you want to do is make money, the very last thing you need is imagination. Or women, for that matter: or men.

"A very good night, Señorita!" cried the patriarch of the house, and Fonny and I were in the streets again, walking.

"Come and see my pad," said Fonny. "It ain't far."

It was getting to be between ten and eleven.

"Okay," I said.

I didn't know the Village, then—I do, now; then, everything was surprising. Where we were walking was much darker and quieter than on Sixth Avenue. We were near the river, and we were the only people in the street. I would have been afraid to walk this street alone.

I had the feeling that I maybe should call home, and I started to say this to Fonny, but I didn't.

His pad was in a basement on Bank Street. We stopped beside a low, black metal railing, with spikes. Fonny opened a gate, very quietly. We walked down four steps, we turned left, facing a door. There were two windows to the right of us. Fonny put his key in the lock, and the door swung inside. There was a weak yellow light above us. Fonny pushed me in before him and closed the door behind us and led me a few paces down a dark, narrow hall. He opened another door, and switched on the light.

It was a small, low room, those were the windows facing the gate. It had a fireplace. Just off the room was a tiny kitchenette and a bathroom. There was a shower; there wasn't any bathtub. In the room, there was a wooden stool and a couple of hassocks and a large wooden table and a small one. On the small table, there were a couple of empty beer cans and on the large table, tools. The room smelled of wood and there was raw wood all over the room. In the far corner, there was a mattress on the floor, covered with a Mexican shawl. There were Fonny's pencil sketches pinned on the wall, and a photograph of Frank.

We were to spend a long time in this room: our lives.

When the doorbell rang, it was Ernestine who went to the door, and Mrs. Hunt who entered first. She was dressed in something which looked very stylish until you looked at it. It was brown, it was shiny, it made one think of satin; and it had somehow white lace fringes at the knees, I think, and the elbows, and—I think—at the waist; and she was wearing a kind of scoop hat, an upside down coal scuttle, which hardened her hard brow.

She was wearing heels, she was gaining weight. She was fighting it, not successfully. She was frightened: in spite of the power of the Holy Ghost. She entered smiling, not quite knowing at what, or at whom, being juggled, so to speak, between the scrutiny of the Holy Ghost and her unsteady recollection of her mirror. And something in the way that she walked in and held out her hand, something in that smile of hers, which begged for mercy at the same time that it could not give it, made her quite wonderful for me. She was a woman I had never seen before. Fonny had been in her belly. She had carried him.

Behind her, were the sisters, who were quite another matter. Ernestine, very hearty and upbeat at the door ("Only way to get to see you people is to call an emergency summit meeting! Now, don't you know that ain't right? Come on *in* this house!") had shuttled Mrs. Hunt past her, into Sharon's orbit: and Sharon, full of grace, delivered her, not quite, to Joseph, who had his arm around me. Something in the way my father held me and something in his smile frightened Mrs. Hunt. But I began to see that she had always been frightened.

Though the sisters were Fonny's sisters, I had never thought of them as his sisters. Well. That's not true. If they had not been Fonny's sisters, I would never have noticed them at all. Because they were his sisters, and I knew that they didn't really like Fonny, I hated them. *They* didn't hate *me*. They didn't hate anybody, and that was what was wrong with them. They smiled at an invisible host of stricken lovers as they entered our living room, and Adrienne, the oldest, who was twenty-seven, and Sheila, who was twenty-four, went out of their way to be very sweet with raggedy-assed me, just like the missionaries had told them. All they really saw was that big black hand of my father's which held them at the waist—of course, my Daddy was really holding *me* at the waist, but it was somehow like it was them. They did not know whether they disapproved of its color, its position, or its shape: but they certainly disapproved of its power of touch. Adrienne was too old for what she was wearing, and Sheila was too young. Behind them, here came Frank, and my father loosened his hold on me a little. We clattered and chattered into the living room.

Mr. Hunt looked very tired, but he still had that smile. He sat down on the sofa, near Adrienne, and he said, "So you saw my big-headed boy today, did you?"

"Yes. He's fine. He sends his love."

"They ain't giving him too hard a time?—I just ask you like that because, you know, he might say things to you he wouldn't say to me."

"Lovers' secrets," said Adrienne, and crossed her legs, and smiled.

I didn't see any reason at all to deal with Adrienne, at least not yet; neither did Mr. Hunt, who kept watching me.

I said, "Well. He hates it, you can see that. And he should. But he's very strong. And he's doing a lot of reading and studying." I looked at Adrienne. "He'll be all right. But we have to get him out of there."

Frank was about to say something when Sheila said, sharply, "If he'd done his reading and studying when he should have, he wouldn't be *in* there."

I started to say something, but Joseph said, quickly, "You bring that six-pack, man? Or, I got some gin and we got whiskey and we got some brandy." He grinned. "Ain't got no Thunderbird, though." He turned to Mrs. Hunt. "I'm sure you ladies won't mind—?"

Mrs. Hunt smiled. "Mind? Frank does not care if we

mind. He will go right on and do what pleases *him*. He ain't never thought about nobody else."

"Mrs. Hunt," said Sharon, "what can I get you, sugar? I can offer you some tea, or coffee—and we got ice cream —and Coca-Cola."

"—and Seven-Up," said Ernestine. "I can make you a kind of ice-cream soda. Come on, Sheila, you want to help me? Sit down, Mama. We'll get it together."

She dragged Sheila into the kitchen.

Mama sat down next to Mrs. Hunt.

"Lord," she said, "the time sure flies. We ain't hardly seen each other since this trouble started."

"Don't say a *word*. I have been running myself *sick*, all up and down the Bronx, trying to get the very best legal advice I can *find*—from some of the people I used to work for, you know—one of them is a city *council*man and he knows just *everybody* and he can *pull* some strings—people just *got* to listen to him, you know. But it's been taking up *all* of my time and the doctor says I *must* be careful, he says I'm putting an awful strain on my heart. He says, Mrs. Hunt, you got to remember, don't care how much that boy wants his freedom, he wants his mother, too. But, look like, it don't matter to me. I ain't worried about *me*. The *Lord* holds *me* up. I just pray and pray and pray that the Lord will bring my boy to the light. That's all I pray for, every day and every night. And then, sometimes I think that maybe this is the *Lord*'s way of making my boy think on his sins and surrender his soul to Jesus—"

"You might be right," said Sharon. "The Lord sure works in mysterious ways."

"Oh, *yes!*" said Mrs. Hunt. "Now, He may *try* you. But He ain't never left none of His children alone."

"What you think," Sharon asked, "of the lawyer, Mr. Hayward, that Ernestine found?"

"I haven't seen him yet. I just have not had time to get downtown. But I know Frank saw him——"

"What do you think, Frank?" Sharon asked.

Frank shrugged. "It's a white boy who's been to a law school and he got them degrees. Well, you know. I ain't got to tell you what that means: it don't mean shit."

"Frank, you're talking to a woman," said Mrs. Hunt.

"I'm hip, and it's a mighty welcome change—like I was saying, it don't mean shit and I ain't sure we're going to stay with him. On the other hand, as white boys go, he's not so bad. He's not as full of shit now, because he's hungry, as he may be later, when he's full. Man," he said to Joseph, "you know I don't want my boy's life in the hands of these white, ball-less motherfuckers. I swear to Christ, I'd rather be boiled alive. That's my only son, man *my only son.* But we all in the hands of white men and I know some very hincty black cats I wouldn't trust, neither."

"But I keep trying to tell you, I keep trying to *tell* you," cried Mrs. Hunt, "that it's that negative attitude which is so dangerous! You're so full of *hate!* If you give people hatred, they will give it back to you! Every time I hear you talk this way, my heart breaks and I tremble for my son, sitting in a dungeon which only the love of

God can bring him out of—Frank, if you love your son, give up this hatred, give it up. It will fall on your son's head, it will kill him."

"Frank's not talking hatred, Mrs. Hunt," Sharon said. "He's just telling the truth about life in this country, and it's only natural for him to be upset."

"I trust in God," said Mrs. Hunt. "I know He cares for me."

"I don't know," Frank said, "how God expects a man to act when his son is in trouble. *Your* God crucified *His* son and was probably glad to get rid of him, but I ain't like that. I ain't hardly going out in the street and kiss the first white cop I see. But I'll be a *very* loving motherfucker the day my son walks out of that hellhole, free. I'll be a *loving* motherfucker when I hold my son's head between my hands again, and look into his eyes. Oh! I'll be *full* of love, *that* day!" He rose from the sofa, and walked over to his wife. "And if it don't go down like that, you can bet I'm going to blow some heads off. And if you say a word to me about that Jesus you been making it with all these years, I'll blow your head off first. You was making it with that white Jew bastard when you should have been with your son."

Mrs. Hunt put her head in her hands, and Frank slowly crossed the room again, and sat down.

Adrienne looked at him and she started to speak, but she didn't. I was sitting on the hassock, near my father. Adrienne said, "Mr. Rivers, exactly what is the purpose of this meeting? You haven't called us all the way over here just to watch my father insult my mother?"

"Why not?" I said. "It's Saturday night. You can't tell what people won't do, if they get bored enough. Maybe we just invited you over to liven things up."

"I can believe," she said, "that you're that malicious. But I can't believe you're that stupid."

"I haven't seen you *twice* since your brother went to jail," I said, "and I ain't *never* seen you down at the Tombs. Fonny told me he saw you once, and you was in a hurry then. And you ain't said a word about it on your job, I bet—have you? And you ain't said a word about it to none of them white-collars ex-antipoverty-program pimps and hustlers and faggots you run with, have you? And you sitting on that sofa right now, thinking you finer than Elizabeth Taylor, and all upset because you got some half-honky chump waiting for you somewhere and you done had to take time out to find out something about your brother." Mrs. Hunt was staring at me with terrible eyes. A cold bitter smile played on Frank's lips: he looked down. Adrienne looked at me from a great distance, adding one more tremendous black mark against her brother's name, and, finally, as I had known all along she wished to do, lit a cigarette. She blew the smoke carefully and delicately into the air, and seemed to be resolving, in silence, that she would never again, for *any* reason, allow herself to be trapped among people so unspeakably inferior to herself.

Sheila and Ernestine reentered, Sheila looking rather frightened, Ernestine looked grimly pleased. She served Mrs. Hunt her ice cream, set down a Coke near Adrienne, gave Joseph a beer, gave Frank a Seven-Up, with gin, gave Sheila a Coke, gave Sharon a Seven-Up, with gin, gave me a brandy, and took a highball for herself. "Happy landings," she said cheerfully, and she sat down and everybody else sat down.

There was, then, this funny silence: and everyone was staring at me. I felt Mrs. Hunt's eyes, more malevolent, more frightened, than ever. She was leaning forward, one hand tight on the spoon buried in her ice cream. Sheila looked terrified. Adrienne's lips curled in a contemptuous smile, and she leaned forward to speak, but her father's hand, hostile, menacing, rose to check her. She leaned back. Frank leaned forward.

My news was, after all, for him. And, looking at him, I said, "I called this summit meeting. I had Daddy ask you all to come over so I could tell you what I had to tell Fonny this afternoon. Fonny's going to be a father. We're going to have a baby."

Frank's eyes left mine, to search my father's. Both men then went away from us, sitting perfectly still, on the chair, on the sofa: they went away together, and they made a strange journey. Frank's face, on this journey, was awful, in the Biblical sense. He was picking up stones and putting them down, his sight forced itself to stretch itself, beyond horizons he had never dreamed of. When he returned, still in company with my father, his face was very peaceful. "You and me going to go out and get drunk," he told Joseph. Then he grinned, looking, almost, just like Fonny, and he said, "I'm glad, Tish. I'm mighty glad."

"And who," asked Mrs. Hunt, "is going to be responsible for this baby?"

"The father and the mother," I said.

Mrs. Hunt stared at me.

"You can bet," Frank said, "that it won't be the Holy Ghost."

Mrs. Hunt stared at Frank, then rose, and started walking toward me; walking very slowly, and seeming to hold her breath. I stood up, and moved to the center of the room, holding mine.

"I guess you call your lustful action love," she said. "I don't. I always knew that you would be the destruction of my son. You have a demon in you—I always knew it. My God caused me to know it many a year ago. The Holy Ghost will cause that child to shrivel in your womb. But my son will be forgiven. *My* prayers will save him."

She was ridiculous and majestic; she was testifying. But Frank laughed and walked over to her, and, with the back of his hand, knocked her down. Yes. She was on the floor, her hat way on the back of her head and her dress up above her knees and Frank stood over her. She did not make a sound, nor did he.

"Her *heart!*" murmured Sharon; and Frank laughed again.

He said, "I think you'll find it's still pumping. But I wouldn't call it a heart." He turned to my father. "Joe, let the women take care of her, and come with me." And, as my father hesitated, "Please. Please, Joe. Come on."

"Go on with him," Sharon said. "Go on."

Sheila knelt beside her mother. Adrienne stubbed out

her cigarette in the ashtray, and stood up. Ernestine came out of the bathroom with rubbing alcohol and knelt beside Sheila. She poured the alcohol onto the cotton and rubbed Mrs. Hunt's temples and forehead, carefully taking the hat completely off and handing it to Sheila.

"Go on, Joe," said Sharon. "We don't need you here."

The two men walked out, the door closed behind them, and now there were these six women who had to deal with each other, if only for a moment. Mrs. Hunt slowly stood up and moved to her chair and sat down. And before she could say anything, I said, "That was a terrible thing you said to me. It was the most terrible thing I've heard in all my life."

"My father didn't have to slap her," said Adrienne. "She *does* have a weak heart."

"She got a weak head," said Sharon. She said to Mrs. Hunt, "The Holy Ghost done softened your brain, child. Did you forget it was Frank's grandchild you was cursing? And of course it's *my* grandchild, too. I know some men and some women would have cut that weak heart out of your body and gladly gone to hell to pay for it. You want some tea, or something? You really ought to have some brandy, but I reckon you too holy for that."

"I don't think you have the right to sneer at my mother's faith," said Sheila.

"Oh, don't give me that bullshit," Ernestine said. "You so shamed you got a Holy Roller for a mother, you don't know what to do. You don't sneer. You just say it shows she's got 'soul,' so other people won't think it's catching

—and also so they'll see what a bright, bright girl *you* are. You make me sick."

"*You* make *me* sick," said Adrienne. "Maybe my mother didn't say it exactly like she *should* have said it—after all, she's very upset! And she *does* have soul! And what do you funky niggers think *you've* got? She only asked one question, *really*—" She put up one hand to keep Ernestine from interrupting her—"She said, Who's going to raise this baby? And who *is*? Tish ain't got no education and God knows she ain't got nothing else and Fonny ain't *never* been worth a damn. You know that yourself. Now. Who *is* going to take care of this baby?"

"*I* am," I said, "you dried up yellow cunt, and you keep on talking, I'm going to take mighty good care of *you*."

She put her hands on her hips, the fool, and Ernestine moved between us, and said, very sweetly, "Adrienne? Baby? May I tell you something, lumps? Sweetie? Sweetie-pie?" She put one hand very lightly against Adrienne's cheek. Adrienne quivered but did not move. Ernestine let her hand rest and play for a moment. "Oh, sugar. From the very first day I laid eyes on your fine person, I got hung up on your Adam's apple. I been dreaming about it. You know what I mean—? When you get hung up on something? You ain't never really been hung up on anything or anybody, have you? You ain't never watched your Adam's apple move, have you? *I* have. I'm watching it right now. Oh. It's delicious. I just can't tell, sweetie, if I want to tear it out with my fingers or my teeth—ooh!—or carve it out, the way you carve a stone from a peach. It is a thing of *beauty*. Can you dig where I'm coming from, sugar?—But if you touch my sister, I'm going to have to make up my mind pretty quick. So"—she moved away from Adrienne —"touch her. Go on, please. Take these chains from my heart and set me free."

"I knew we shouldn't have come," Sheila said. "I knew it."

Ernestine stared at Sheila until Sheila was forced to raise her eyes. Then, Ernestine laughed, and said, "My. I must have a dirty mind, Sheila. I didn't know that you could even *say* that word."

Then real hatred choked off the air. Something bottomless occurred which had nothing to do with what seemed to be occurring in the room. I suddenly felt sorry for the sisters—but Ernestine didn't. She stood where she stood, one hand on her waist, one hand hanging free, moving only her eyes. She was wearing gray slacks and an old blouse and her hair was untidy on her head and she wore no makeup. She was smiling. Sheila looked as though she could hardly breathe or stand, as though she wanted to run to her mother, who had not moved from her chair. Adrienne, whose hips were wide, wore a white blouse and a black, flaring, pleated skirt and a short, tight, black jacket and low heels. Her hair was parted in the middle and tied with a white ribbon at the nape of her neck. Her hands were no longer on her hips. Her skin, which was just a shade too dark to be high yellow, had darkened and mottled. Her forehead seemed covered with oil. Her eyes had darkened with her skin and the skin was rejecting the makeup by denying it any moisture. One saw that she was not really very pretty, that the face and the body would coarsen and thicken with time.

"Come," she said to Sheila, "away from these foul-mouthed people," and she had a certain dignity as she said it.

They both walked to their mother, who was, I could suddenly see, the witness to, and guardian of their chastity.

Mrs. Hunt rose, then, oddly peaceful.

"I sure hope," she said, "that you're pleased with the way you raised your daughters, Mrs. Rivers."

Sharon was peaceful, too, but there was a kind of startled wonder in it: she stared at Mrs. Hunt and said nothing. And Mrs. Hunt added, "These girls won't be bringing *me* no bastards to feed, I can guarantee you that."

"But the child that's coming," said Sharon, after a moment, "is your grandchild. I don't understand you. It's your *grandchild*. What difference does it make how it gets here? The child ain't got nothing to do with that —don't none of us have nothing to do with *that!*"

"That child," said Mrs. Hunt, and she looked at me for a moment, then started for the door, Sharon watching her all the while, "that child——"

I let her get to the door. My mother moved, but as though in a dream, to swing the locks; but I got there before her; I put my back against the door. Adrienne and Sheila were behind their mother.

Sharon and Ernestine did not move.

"That child," I said, "is in my belly. Now, you raise your knee and kick it out—or with them high heel shoes. You don't want this child? Come on and kill it now. I dare you." I looked her in the eyes. "It won't be the first child you tried to kill." I touched her upside down coal scuttle hat. I looked at Adrienne and Sheila. "You did pretty well with the first two—" and then I opened the door, but I didn't move—"okay, you try it again, with Fonny. I dare you."

"May we," asked Adrienne, with what she hoped was ice in her voice, "leave now?"

"Tish," said Sharon; but she did not move.

Ernestine moved past me, moving me away from the door and delivering me to Sharon. "Ladies," she said, and moved to the elevator and pressed the button. She was past a certain fury now. When the elevator arrived and the door opened, she merely said, ushering them in, but holding the door open with one shoulder, "Don't worry. We'll never tell the baby about you. There's no way to tell a baby how obscene human beings can be!" And, in another tone of voice, a tone I'd never heard before, she said, to Mrs. Hunt, "Blessed be the next fruit of thy womb. I hope it turns out to be uterine cancer. And I mean that." And, to the sisters, "If you come anywhere near this house again in life, *I will kill you.* This child is not your child—you have just said so. If I hear that you have so much as crossed a playground and *seen* the child, you won't live to get any *kind* of cancer. Now. I am not my sister. Remember that. My sister's nice. I'm not. My father and my mother are nice. I'm not. I can tell you why Adrienne can't get fucked—you want to hear it? I could tell you about Sheila, too, and all those cats she jerks off in their handkerchiefs, in cars and movies—now, you want to hear *that?*" Sheila began to cry and Mrs. Hunt moved to close the elevator door. Ernestine laughed, and, with one shoulder, held it open and her voice changed again. "You just cursed the child in my sister's womb. Don't you *never* let me see you again, you broken down half-white bride of Christ!" And she spat in Mrs. Hunt's face, and then let the elevator door close. And she yelled down the shaft, "That's your flesh and blood you were cursing, you sick, filthy dried-up cunt! And you carry that message to the Holy Ghost and if He don't like it you tell Him I said He's a faggot and He better not come nowhere near me."

And she came back into the house, with tears running down her face, and walked to the table and poured herself a drink. She lit a cigarette; she was trembling.

Sharon, in all this, had said nothing. Ernestine had delivered me to her, but Sharon had not, in fact, touched me. She had done something far more tremendous; which was, mightily, to hold me and keep me still; without touching me.

"Well," she said, "the men are going to be out for a while. And Tish needs her rest. So let's go on to sleep."

But I knew that they were sending me to bed so that they could sit up for a while, without me, without the men, without anybody, to look squarely in the face the fact that Fonny's family didn't give a shit about him and were not going to do a thing to help him. *We* were his family now, the only family he had: and now everything was up to us.

I walked into my bedroom very slowly and I sat down on the bed for a minute. I was too tired to cry. I was too tired to feel anything. In a way, Sis Ernestine had taken it all on herself, everything, because she wanted the child to make its journey safely and get here well: and that meant that I had to sleep.

So I undressed and curled up on the bed. I turned the way I'd always turned toward Fonny, when we were in bed together. I crawled into his arms and he held me. And he was so present for me that, again, I could not cry. My tears would have hurt him too much. So he held me and I whispered his name, while I watched the streetlights playing on the ceiling. Dimly, I could hear Mama and Sis in the kitchen, making believe that they were playing gin rummy.

That night, in the room on Bank Street, Fonny took the Mexican shawl off the pallet he had on the floor and draped it over my head and shoulders. He grinned and stepped back. "I be damned," he said, "there *is* a rose in Spanish Harlem." He grinned again. "Next week, I'm going to get you a rose for your hair." Then, he stopped grinning and a kind of stinging silence filled the room and filled my ears. It was like nothing was happening in the world but us. I was not afraid. It was deeper than fear. I could not take my eyes away from his. I could

not move. If it was deeper than fear, it was not yet joy.
It was wonder.

He said, not moving, "We're grown up now, you
know?"

I nodded.

He said, "And you've always been—*mine*—no?"

I nodded again.

"And you know," he said, still not moving, holding me
with those eyes, "that I've always been yours, right?"

I said, "I never thought about it that way."

He said, "Think about it now, Tish."

"I just know that I love you," I said, and I started to
cry. The shawl seemed very heavy and hot and I wanted
to take it off, but I couldn't.

Then he moved, his face changed, he came to me and
took the shawl away and flung it into a corner. He took
me in his arms and he kissed my tears and then he kissed
me and then we both knew something which we had not
known before.

"I love you, too," he said, "but *I* try not to cry about it."
He laughed and he made me laugh and then he kissed
me again, harder, and he stopped laughing. "I want you
to marry me," he said. I must have looked surprised, for
he said, "That's right. I'm yours and you're mine and
that's it, baby. But I've got to try to explain something to
you."

He took me by the hand and led me to his worktable.

"This is where my life is," he said, "my real life." He
picked up a small piece of wood, it was about the size
of two fists. There was the hope of an eye gouged into it,

the suggestion of a nose—the rest was simply a lump of somehow breathing wood. "This might turn out all right one day," he said, and laid it gently down. "But I think I might already have fucked it up." He picked up another piece, the size of a man's thigh. A woman's torso was trapped in it. "I don't know a thing about her yet," he said, and put it down, again very gently. Though he held me by one shoulder and was very close to me, he was yet very far away. He looked at me with his little smile. "Now, listen," he said, "I ain't the kind of joker going to give you a hard time running around after other chicks and shit like that. I smoke a little pot but I ain't never popped no needles and I'm really very square. But—" he stopped and looked at me, very quiet, very hard: there was a hardness in him I had barely sensed before. Within this hardness moved his love, moved as a torrent or as a fire moves, above reason, beyond argument, not to be modified in any degree by anything life might do. I was his, and he was mine—I suddenly realized that I would be a very unlucky and perhaps a dead girl should I ever attempt to challenge this decree.

"But," he continued—and he moved away from me; his heavy hands seemed to be attempting to shape the air—"I live with wood and stone. I got stone in the basement and I'm working up here all the time and I'm looking for a loft where I can really work. So, all I'm trying to tell you, Tish, is I ain't offering you much. I ain't got no money and I work at odd jobs—just for bread, because I ain't about to go for none of their jive-ass okey-doke—and that means that you going to have to work, too, and when you come home most likely I'll just grunt and keep on with my chisels and shit and maybe sometimes you'll think I don't even know you're there. But don't ever think that, ever. You're with me all the time, all the time, without you I don't know if I could make it at all, baby, and when I put down the chisel, I'll always come to you. I'll always come to you. I need you. I love you." He smiled. "Is that all right, Tish?"

"Of course it's all right with me," I said. I had more to say, but my throat wouldn't open.

He took me by the hand, then, and he led me to the pallet on the floor. He sat down beside me, and he pulled me down so that my face was just beneath his, my head was in his lap. I sensed a certain terror in him. He knew that I could feel his sex stiffening and beginning to rage against the cloth of his pants and against my jawbone; he wanted me to feel it, and yet he was afraid. He kissed my face all over, and my neck, and he uncovered my breasts and put his teeth and tongue there and his hands were all over my body. I knew what he was doing, and I didn't know. I was in his hands, he called me by the thunder at my ear. I was in his hands: I was being changed; all that I could do was cling to him. I did not realize, until I realized it, that I was also kissing him, that everything was breaking and changing and turning in me and moving toward him. If his arms had not held me, I would have fallen straight downward, backward, to my death. My life was holding me. My life was claiming me. I heard, I felt his breath, as for the first time: but it was as though his breath were rising up out of me. He opened my legs, or I opened them, and he kissed the inside of my thighs. He took off all my clothes, he covered my whole body with kisses, and then he covered me with the shawl and then he went away.

The shawl scratched. I was cold and hot. I heard him in the bathroom. I heard him pull the chain. When he came back, he was naked. He got under the shawl, with me, and stretched his long body on top of mine, and I felt his long black heavy sex throbbing against my navel.

He took my face in his hands, and held it, and he kissed me.

"Now, don't be scared," he whispered. "Don't be scared. Just remember that I belong to you. Just remember that I wouldn't hurt you for nothing in this world. You just going to have to get used to me. And we got all the time in the world."

It was getting to be between two and three: he read my mind. "Your Mama and Daddy know you're with me," he said, "and they know I won't let nothing happen to you." Then, he moved down and his sex moved against my opening. "Don't be scared," he said again. "Hold on to me."

I held on to him, in an agony; there was nothing else in the world to hold on to; I held him by his nappy hair. I could not tell if he moaned or if I moaned. It hurt, it hurt, it didn't hurt. It was a strange weight, a presence coming into me—into a me I had not known was there. I almost screamed, I started to cry: it hurt. It didn't hurt.

Something began, unknown. His tongue, his teeth on my breasts, hurt. I wanted to throw him off, I held him tighter and still he moved and moved and moved. I had not known there was so much of him. I screamed and cried against his shoulder. He paused. He put both hands beneath my hips. He moved back, but not quite out, I hung nowhere for a moment, then he pulled me against him and thrust in with all his might and something broke in me. Something broke and a scream rose up in me but he covered my lips with his lips, he strangled my scream with his tongue. His breath was in my nostrils, I was breathing with his breath and moving with his body. And now I was open and helpless and I felt him everywhere. A singing began in me and his body became sacred—his buttocks, as they quivered and rose and fell, and his thighs between my thighs and the weight of his chest on mine and that stiffness of his which stiffened and grew and throbbed and brought me to another place. I wanted to laugh and cry. Then, something absolutely new began, I laughed and I cried and I called his name. I held him closer and closer and I strained to receive it all, all, all of him. He paused and he kissed me and kissed me. His head moved all over my neck and my breasts. We could hardly breathe: if we did not breathe again soon, I knew we would die. Fonny moved again, at first very slowly, and then faster and faster. I felt it coming, felt myself coming, going over the edge, everything in me flowing down to him, and I called his name over and over while he growled my name in his throat, thrusting now with no mercy—

caught his breath sharply, let it out with a rush and a sob and then pulled out of me, holding me tight, shooting a boiling liquid all over my belly and my chest and my chin.

Then we lay still, glued together, for a long time.

"I'm sorry," he said, finally, shyly, into the long silence, "to have made such a mess. But I guess you don't want to have no baby right away and I didn't have no protection on me."

"I think I made a mess, too," I said. "It was the first time. Isn't there supposed to be blood?"

We were whispering. He laughed a little. "I had a hemorrhage. Shall we look?"

"I like lying here like this, with you."

"I do too." Then, "Do you like me, Tish?" He sounded like a little boy. "I mean—when I make love to you—do you like it?"

I said, "Oh, come on. You just want to hear me say it."

"That's true. So—?"

"So what?"

"So why don't you go ahead and say it?" And he kissed me.

I said, "It was a little bit like being hit by a truck"— he laughed again—"but it was the most beautiful thing that ever happened to me."

"For me, too," he said. He said it in a very wondering way, almost as though he were speaking of someone else. "No one ever loved me like that before."

"Have you had a lot of girls?"

"Not so many. And nobody for you to worry about."

"Do I know any of them?"

He laughed. "You want me to walk you down the street and point them out to you? Now, you know that wouldn't be nice. And, now that I've got to know you just a little better, I don't believe it would be safe." He snuggled up to me and put his hand on my breast. "You got a wildcat in you, girl. Even if I had the time to go running after other foxes, I sure wouldn't have the energy. I'm really going to have to start taking my vitamins."

"Oh, shut up. You're disgusting."

"Why am I disgusting? I'm only talking about my *health*. Don't you care nothing about my *health*? And they're *chocolate covered*—vitamins, I mean."

"You're crazy."

"Well," he conceded cheerfully, "I'm crazy about you. You want we should check the damage before this stuff hardens into cement?"

He turned on the light and we looked down at ourselves and our bed.

Well, we were something of a sight. There was blood, quite a lot of it—or it seemed like a lot to me, but it didn't frighten me at all, I felt proud and happy—on him and on the bed and on me; his sperm and my blood were slowly creeping down my body, and his sperm was on him and on me; and, in the dim light and against our dark bodies, the effect was as of some strange anointing. Or, we might have just completed a tribal rite. And Fonny's body was a total mystery to me—the body of one's lover always is, no matter how well one gets to know it:

it is the changing envelope which contains the gravest mystery of one's life. I stared at his heavy chest, his flat belly, the belly button, the spinning black hair, the heavy limp sex: he had never been circumcized. I touched his slim body and I kissed him on the chest. It tasted of salt and some pungent, unknown bitter spice—clearly, as others might put it, it would become an acquired taste. One hand on my hand, one hand on my shoulder, he held me very close. Then he said, "We've got to go. I better get you home before dawn."

It was half past four.

"I guess so," I said, and we got up and walked into the shower. I washed his body and he washed mine and we laughed a lot, like children, and he warned me if I didn't take my hands off him we might never get uptown and then my Daddy might jump salty and, after all, Fonny said, he had a lot to talk to my Daddy about and he had to talk to him right away.

Fonny got me home at seven. He held me in his arms in the almost empty subway all the way uptown. It was Sunday morning. We walked our streets together, hand in hand; not even the church people were up yet; and the people who were still up, the few people, didn't have eyes for us, didn't have eyes for anybody, or anything.

We got to my stoop and I thought Fonny would leave me there and I turned to kiss him away, but he took me by the hand and said, "Come on," and we walked up the stairs. Fonny knocked on the door.

Sis opened it, her hair tied up, wearing an old green bathrobe. She looked as evil as she could be. She looked from me to Fonny and back again. She didn't exactly want to, but she smiled.

"You're just in time for coffee," she said, and moved back from the door, to let us in.

"We——" I started to say; but Fonny said, "Good-morning, Miss Rivers"—and something in his tone made Sis look at him sharply and come full awake—"I'm sorry we coming in so late. Can I speak to Mr. Rivers, please? It's important."

He still held me by the hand.

"It might be easier to see him," Sis said, "if you come inside, out of the hall."

"We——" I started again, intending to make up God knows what excuse.

"Want to get married," Fonny said.

"Then you'd really better have some coffee," Sis said, and closed the door behind us.

Sharon now came into the kitchen, and she was some-what more together than Sis—that is, she was wearing slacks, and a sweater, and she had knotted her hair in one braid and skewered it to the top of her skull.

"Now, where have you two been," she began, "till this hour of the morning? Don't you know better than to be behaving like that? I declare. We was just about to start calling the police."

But I could see, too, that she was relieved that Fonny was sitting in the kitchen, beside me. That meant some-thing very important, and she knew it. It would have been a very different scene, and she would have been in very different trouble if I had come upstairs alone.

"I'm sorry, Mrs. Rivers," Fonny said. "It's all my fault. I hadn't seen Tish for a few weeks and we had a lot to talk about—*I* had a lot to talk about—and—" he gestured—"I kept her out."

"Talking?" Sharon asked.

He did not quite flinch; he did not drop his eyes. "We want to get married," he said. "That's how come I kept her out so late." They watched each other. "I love Tish," he said. "That's why I stayed away so long. I even—" he looked briefly at me—"went to see other girls—and—I did all kind of things, to kind of get it out of my mind." He looked at me again. He looked down. "But I could see I was just fooling myself. I didn't love nobody else but her. And then I got scared that maybe she'd go away or somebody else would come along and take her away and so I came back." He tried to grin. "I came running back. And I don't want to have to go away again." Then, "She's always been my girl, you know that. And—I am not a bad boy. You know that. And—you're the only family I've ever had."

"That," Sharon grumbled, "is why I can't figure out why you calling me Mrs. Rivers, all of a sudden." She looked at me. "Yeah. I hope you realize, Miss, that you ain't but eighteen years old."

"*That* argument," said Sis, "and a subway token, will get you from here to the corner. If *that* far!" She poured the coffee. "Actually, it's the older sister who is expected to marry first. But we have never stood on ceremony in *this* house."

"What do *you* think about all this?" Sharon asked her.

"Me? I'm delighted to be rid of the little brat. I never *could* stand her. I *could* never see what all the rest of you saw in her, I swear." She sat down at the table and grinned. "Take some sugar, Fonny. You are going to need it, believe me, if you intend to tie yourself up with my sweet, *sweet* little sister."

Sharon went to the kitchen door, and yelled, "Joe! Come on out here! Lightning's done struck the poorhouse! Come on, now, I mean it."

Fonny took my hand.

Joseph came into the kitchen, in slippers, old corduroy pants, and a T-shirt. I began to realize that no one in this house had really been to sleep. Joseph saw me first. He really did not see anyone else. And, since he was both furious and relieved, his tone was very measured. "I'd like you to tell me exactly what you mean, young lady, by walking in here this hour of the morning. If you want to leave home, then you leave home, you hear? But, as long as you in *my* house, you got to respect it. You hear me?"

Then he saw Fonny, and Fonny let go my hand, and stood up.

He said, "Mr. Rivers, please don't scold Tish. It's all my fault, sir. I kept her out. I had to talk to her. Please. Mr. Rivers. Please. I asked her to marry me. That's what we were doing out so long. We want to get married. That's why I'm here. You're her father. You love her. And so I know you know—you *have* to know—that I love her. I've loved her all my life. You know that. And if I didn't love her, I wouldn't be standing in this room now—would I? I could have left her on the stoop and run away again. I know you might want to beat me up. But I love her. That's all I can tell you."

Joseph looked at him.

"How old are you?"

"I'm twenty-one, sir."

"You think that's old enough to get married?"

"I don't know, sir. But it's old enough to know who you love."

"You think so?"

Fonny straightened. "I know so."

"How you going to feed her?"

"How did you?"

We, the women, were out of it now, and we knew it. Ernestine poured Joseph a cup of coffee and pushed it in his direction.

"You got a job?"

"I load moving vans in the daytime and I sculpt at night. I'm a sculptor. We know it won't be easy. But I'm a real artist. And I'm going to be a very good artist— maybe, even, a great one." And they stared at each other again.

Joseph picked up his coffee, without looking at it, and sipped it without tasting it.

"Now, let me get this straight. You asked my little girl to marry you, and she said——"

"Yes," said Fonny.

"And you come here to tell me or to ask my permission?"

"Both, sir," said Fonny.

"And you ain't got no kind of——"

"Future," Fonny said.

Both men, again, then measured each other. Joseph put his coffee down. Fonny had not touched his.

"What would you do in my place?" Joseph asked.

I could feel Fonny trembling. He could not help it—his hand touched my shoulder lightly, then moved away. "I'd ask my daughter. If she tells you she don't love me, I'll go away and I won't never bother you no more."

Joseph looked hard at Fonny—a long look, in which one watched skepticism surrender to a certain resigned tenderness, a self-recognition. He looked as though he wanted to knock Fonny down; he looked as though he wanted to take him in his arms.

Then Joseph looked at me.

"Do you love him? You want to marry him?"

"Yes." I had not known my voice could sound so strange. "Yes. Yes." Then, I said, "I'm very much your daughter, you know, and very much my mother's daughter. So, you ought to know that I mean no when I say no and I mean yes when I say yes. And Fonny came here to ask for your permission, and I love him for that. I very much want your permission because I love you. But I am not going to marry *you*. I am going to marry Fonny."

Joseph sat down.

"When?"

"As soon as we get the bread together," Fonny said.

Joseph said, "You and me, son, we better go into the other room."

And so they went away. We did not say anything.

There was nothing for us to say. Only, Mama said, after a moment, "You sure you love him, Tish? You're sure?"

"Mama," I said, "why do you ask me that?"

"Because she's been secretly hoping that you'd marry Governor Rockefeller," Ernestine said.

For a moment Mama looked at her, hard; then she laughed. Ernestine, without knowing it, or meaning to, had come very close to the truth—not the literal truth, but the truth: for the dream of safety dies hard. I said, "You know that dried-up cracker ass-hole is much too old for me."

Sharon laughed again. "That is not," she said, "the way he sees *himself*. But I guess I just would not be able to swallow the way he would see *you*. So. We can close the subject. You going to marry Fonny. All right. When I really think about it"—and now she paused, and, in a way, she was no longer Sharon, my mother, but someone else; but that someone else was, precisely, my mother, Sharon—"I guess I'm real pleased." She leaned back, arms folded, looking away, thinking ahead. "Yeah. He's real. He's a man."

"He's not a man yet," said Ernestine, "but he's going to become a man—that's why you sitting there, fighting them tears. Because that means that your youngest daughter is about to become a woman."

"Oh, shut up," Sharon said. "Wish to God you'd get married to somebody, then I'd be able to bug *you* half to death, instead of the other way around."

"You'd miss me, too," said Ernestine, very quietly, "but I don't think I'm ever going to marry. Some peo-

ple do, you know—Mama?—and some people don't."
She stood up and kind of circled the room and sat down
again. We could hear Fonny's voice and Joseph's voice,
in the other room, but we couldn't hear what they were
saying—also, we were trying very hard *not* to hear. Men
are men, and sometimes they must be left alone. Especially if you have the sense to realize that if they're
locked in a room together, where they may not especially want to be, they are locked in because of their
responsibility for the women outside.

"Well I can understand that," said Sharon—very steadily, and without moving.

"The only trouble," Ernestine said, "is that sometimes
you would *like* to belong to somebody."

"But," I said—I had not known I was going to say it
—"it's very frightening to belong to somebody."

And perhaps until the moment I heard myself say
this, I had not realized that this is true.

"Six in one," said Ernestine, and smiled, "half dozen
in the other."

Joseph and Fonny came back from the other room.

"Both of you are crazy," Joseph said, "but there's nothing I can do about *that*." He watched Fonny. He smiled
—a smile both sweet and reluctant. Then, he looked at
me. "But—Fonny's right—somebody was bound to come
along some day and take you away. I just didn't think it
would happen so soon. But—like Fonny says, and it's
true—you've always been together, from childhood on.
And you ain't children no more." He took Fonny by
the hand and led Fonny to me, and he took me by the

hand and he pulled me to my feet. He put my hand in Fonny's hand. "Take care of each other," he said. "You going to find out that it's more than a notion."

Tears were standing in Fonny's eyes. He kissed my father. He let go my hand. He moved to the door. "I've got to get home," he said, "and tell my Daddy." His face changed, he looked at me, he kissed me across the space dividing us. "He'll be mighty happy," he said. He opened the door. He said to Joseph, "We be back here around six this evening, okay?"

"Okay," said Joseph, and now he was smiling all over his face.

Fonny went on out the door. Two or three days later, Tuesday or Wednesday, we went downtown together again and started seriously looking around for our loft.

And *that* was going to turn out to be a trip and a half.

Mr. Hayward was in his office on the Monday, just as he had said he would be. I got there about seven fifteen, and Mama was with me.

Mr. Hayward is about thirty-seven, I would guess, with gentle brown eyes and thinning brown hair. He's very, very tall, and he's big; and he's nice enough, or he seems nice enough, but I'm just not comfortable with him. I don't know if it's fair to blame him for this. I'm not really comfortable with anybody these days, and I guess I certainly wouldn't be comfortable with a lawyer.

He stood up as we came in, and put Mama in the big chair and me in the smaller one and sat down again behind his desk.

"How are you ladies today? Mrs. Rivers? And how are you, Tish? Did you see Fonny?"

"Yes. At six o'clock."

"And how is he?"

That always seemed a foolish question to me. How *is* a man if he's fighting to get out of prison? But then, too, I had to force myself to see, from another point of view, that it was an important question. For one thing, it was the question I was living with; and, for another, knowing "how" Fonny was might make a very important difference for Mr. Hayward, and help him with his case. But I also resented having to tell Mr. Hayward anything at all about Fonny. There was so much that I felt he should already have known. But maybe I'm being unfair about that, too.

"Well, let's put it this way, Mr. Hayward. He hates being in there, but he's trying not to let it break him."

"When we going to get him out?" asked Mama.

Mr. Hayward looked from Mama to me, and smiled— a painful smile, as though he had just been kicked in the balls. He said, "Well, as you ladies know, this is a very difficult case."

"That's why my sister hired *you*," I said.

"And you are beginning to feel now that her confidence was misplaced?" He was still smiling. He lit a cigar.

"No," I said, "I wouldn't say that."

I wouldn't have dared to say that—not yet, anyway— because I was afraid of having to look for another lawyer, who might easily be worse.

"We liked having Fonny around," Mama said, "and we just kind of miss him."

"I can certainly understand that," he said, "and I'm doing all I can to get him back to you, just as fast as I can. But, as you ladies know, the very greatest difficulty has been caused by the refusal of Mrs. Rogers to reconsider her testimony. And now she has disappeared."

"Disappeared?" I shouted, "how can she just disappear?"

"Tish," he said, "this is a very big city, a very big country—even, for that matter, a very big world. People *do* disappear. I don't think that *she* has gone very far—they certainly do not have the means for a long journey. But her family may have returned her to Puerto Rico. In any case, in order to find her, I will need special investigators, and—"

"That means money," Mama said.

"Alas," said Mr. Hayward. He stared at me from behind his cigar, an odd, expectant, surprisingly sorrowful look.

I had stood up; now I sat down. "That filthy bitch," I said, "that filthy bitch."

"How *much* money?" Mama asked.

"I am trying to keep it as low as possible," said Mr. Hayward, with a shy, boyish smile, "but special investigators are—*special*, I'm afraid, and they know it. If we're lucky, we'll locate Mrs. Rogers in a matter of days, or weeks. If not"—he shrugged—"well, for the moment, let's just assume we'll be lucky." And he smiled again.

"Puerto Rico," Mama said heavily.

"We don't *know* that she has returned there," Mr. Hayward said, "but it *is* a very vivid possibility. Anyway, she and her husband disappeared some days ago from the apartment on Orchard Street, leaving no forwarding address. We have not been able to contact the other relatives, the aunts and uncles, who, anyway, as you know, have never been very cooperative."

"But doesn't it make it look bad for her story," I asked, "to just disappear like that? She's the key witness in this case."

"Yes. But she is a distraught, ignorant, Puerto Rican woman, suffering from the aftereffects of rape. So her behavior is not incomprehensible. You see what I mean?" He looked at me hard, and his voice changed. "And she is only *one* of the key witnesses in this case. You have forgotten the testimony of Officer Bell—*his* was the really authoritative identification of the rapist. It is Bell who swears that he *saw* Fonny running away from the scene of the crime. And I have always been of the opinion—you will remember that we discussed this—that it is *his* testimony which Mrs. Rogers continually repeats——"

"If he saw Fonny at the scene of the crime, then why did he have to wait and come and get him out of the *house?*"

"Tish," Mama said. "Tish." Then, "You mean—let me get you straight now—that it's that Officer Bell who tells her what to say? You mean *that?*"

"Yes," said Mr. Hayward.

I looked at Hayward. I looked around the room. We

were way downtown, near Broadway, not far from Trinity Church. The office was of dark wood, very smooth and polished. The desk was wide, with two telephones, a button kept flashing. Hayward ignored it, watching me. There were trophies and diplomas on the walls, and a large photograph of Hayward, Senior. On the desk, framed, were two photographs, one of his wife, smiling, and one of his two small boys. There was no connection between this room, and me.

Yet, here I was.

"You're saying," I said, "that there's no way of getting at the truth in this case?"

"No. I am not saying that." He re-lit his cigar. "The truth of a case doesn't matter. What matters is—who wins."

Cigar smoke filled the room. "I don't mean," he said, carefully, "that I doubt the truth. If I didn't believe in Fonny's innocence, I would never have taken the case. I know something about Officer Bell, who is a racist and a liar—I have told him that to his face, so you can feel perfectly free to quote me, to anyone, at any time you wish—and I know something about the D.A. in charge of this case, who is worse. Now. You and Fonny insist that you were together, in the room on Bank Street, along with an old friend, Daniel Carty. Your testimony, as you can imagine, counts for nothing, and Daniel Carty has just been arrested by the D.A.'s office and is being held incommunicado. I have not been allowed to see him." Now, he rose and paced to the window. "What they are doing is really against the law—but—Daniel has a record, as you know. They, obviously, intend to make him change his testimony. And—I do not *know* this, but I am willing to bet—that that is how and why Mrs. Rogers has disappeared." He paced back to his desk, and sat down. "So. You see." He looked up at me. "I will make it as easy as I can. But it will still be very hard."

"How soon do you need the money?" Mama asked.

"I have begun the operation already," he said, "of tracing the lady. I will need the money as soon as you can get it. I will also force the D.A.'s office to allow me to see Daniel Carty, but they will throw every conceivable obstacle in my way——"

"So we're trying," Mama said, "to buy time."

"Yes," he said.

Time: the word tolled like the bells of a church. Fonny was doing: *time*. In six months *time*, our baby would be here. Somewhere, in time, Fonny and I had met: somewhere, in time, we had loved; somewhere, no longer in time, but, now, totally, at time's mercy, we loved.

Somewhere in time, Fonny paced a prison cell, his hair growing—nappier and nappier. Somewhere, in time, he stroked his chin, itching for a shave, somewhere, in time, he scratched his armpits, aching for a bath. Somewhere in time he looked about him, knowing that he was being lied to, in time, with the connivance of time. In another time, he had feared life: now, he feared death—somewhere in time. He awoke every morning with Tish on his eyelids and fell asleep every night with Tish tormenting his navel. He lived, now, in time, with the

roar and the stink and the beauty and horror of innu-
merable men: and he had been dropped into this inferno in the twinkling of an eye.

Time could not be bought. The only coin time ac-
cepted was life. Sitting on the leather arm of Mr. Hayward's chair, I looked through the vast window, way
down, on Broadway, and I began to cry.

"Tish," said Hayward, helplessly.

Mama came and took me in her arms.

"Don't do us like that," she said. "Don't do us like
that."

But I couldn't stop. It just seemed that we would
never find Mrs. Rogers; that Bell would never change
his testimony; that Daniel would be beaten until he
changed his. And Fonny would rot in prison, Fonny
would die there—and I—I could not live without Fonny.

"Tish," Mama said, "you a woman now. You *got* to
be a woman. We are in a rough situation—but, if you
really want to think about it, ain't nothing new about
that. That's just exactly, daughter, when *you do not give
up.* You *can't* give up. We got to get Fonny out of there.
I don't care what we have to do to do it—you understand
me, daughter? This shit has been going on long enough.
Now. You start thinking about it any other way, you
just going to make yourself sick. *You* can't get sick *now*
—you know that—I'd rather for the state to kill him
than for *you* to kill him. So, come on, now—we going to
get him *out.*"

She moved away from me. I dried my eyes. She
turned back to Hayward.

"You don't have an address for that child in Puerto Rico, do you?"

"Yes." He wrote it out on a piece of paper, and handed it to her. "We're sending somebody down there this week."

Mama folded the piece of paper, and put it in her purse.

"How soon do you think you'll be able to see Daniel?"

"I intend," he said, "to see him tomorrow, but I'm going to have to raise all kinds of hell to do it."

"Well," Mama said, "just as long as you do it."

She came back to me.

"We'll put our heads together, at home, Mr. Hayward, and start working it on out, and I'll have Ernestine call you early tomorrow morning. All right?"

"That's fine. Please give Ernestine my regards." He put down his cigar, and came and put one clumsy hand on my shoulder. "My dear Tish," he said. "Please hold on. Please hold on. I swear to you that we will win, that Fonny will have his freedom. No, it will not be easy. But neither will it be as insurmountable as it seems to you today."

"Tell her," Mama said.

"Now—when I go to see Fonny, the first question he always asks is always about you. And I always say, Tish? she's fine. But he watches my face, to make sure I'm not lying. And I'm a very bad liar. I'm going to see him tomorrow. What shall I tell him?"

I said, "Tell him I'm fine."

"Do you think you can manage to give us a little

smile?—to go with the message. I could carry it with me. He'd like that."

I smiled, and he smiled, and something really human happened between us, for the first time. He released my shoulder, and walked over to Mama. "Could you have Ernestine call me around ten? or even earlier, if possible. Otherwise, she may not be able to get me before six."

"Will do. And thank you very much, Mr. Hayward."

"You know something—? I wish you'd drop the mister."

"Well—okay. Hayward. Call me Sharon."

"That I will do. And I hope that we become friends, out of all this."

"I'm sure we will," Mama said. "Thank you again. 'Bye now."

"Good-bye. Don't forget what I said, Tish."

"I won't. I promise. Tell Fonny I'm fine."

"*That's* my girl. Or, rather"—and he looked more boyish than ever—"Fonny's girl." And he smiled. He opened the door for us. He said, "Good-bye."

We said, "Good-bye."

Fonny had been walking down Seventh Avenue, on a Saturday afternoon, when he ran into Daniel again. They had not seen each other since their days in school.

Time had not improved Daniel. He was still big, black, and loud; at the age of twenty-three—he is a little older than Fonny—he was already running out of familiar faces. So, they grabbed each other on the avenue—after a moment of genuine shock and delight—howling with laughter, beating each other around the head and shoulders, children again, and, though Fonny doesn't like bars, sat themselves down at the nearest one, and ordered two beers.

"Wow! What's happening?" I don't know which of them asked the question, or which of them asked it first: but I can see their faces.

"Why you asking *me*, man?"

"Because, like the man says about Mt. Everest, you're *there*."

"Where?"

"No kidding, man—how you making it?"

"I gotta slave for the Jew in the garment center, pushing a hand truck, man, riding up and down in them elevators."

"How your folks?"

"Oh, my Daddy passed, man, while ago. I'm still at the same place, with my Mama. Her varicose veins come down on her, though. So"—and Daniel looked down into his beer.

"What you doing—I mean, now?"

"You mean, this minute?"

"I mean, you any plans, man, you hung up, or can you come on and hang out with me? I mean, right now—?"

"I ain't doing nothing."

Fonny swallowed his beer, and paid the man. "Come

on. We got some beer at the pad. Come *on*. You remember Tish?"

"Tish?—"

"*Yeah*, Tish. Skinny little Tish. *My* girl."

"Skinny little Tish?"

"*Yeah*. She's *still* my girl. We going to get married, man. Come on, and let me show you the pad. And she'll fix us something to eat—come *on*, I told you we got beer at the house."

And, though he certainly shouldn't be spending the money, he pushes Daniel into a cab and they roll on down to Bank Street: where I am not expecting them. But Fonny is big and cheerful, overjoyed; and the truth is that I recognize Daniel by the light in Fonny's eyes. For, it is not so much that time has not improved him: I can see to what extent he has been beaten. This is not because I am perceptive, but because I am in love with Fonny. Neither love nor terror makes one blind: indifference makes one blind. And I could not be indifferent to Daniel because I realized, from Fonny's face, how marvelous it was for him to have scooped up, miraculously, from the swamp waters of his past, a friend.

But it means that I must go out, shopping, and so out I go, leaving them alone. We have a record player. As I go out, Fonny is putting on "Compared To What," and Daniel is squatting on the floor, drinking beer.

"So, you really going to get married?" Daniel asks —both wistful and mocking.

"Well, yeah, we looking for a place to live—we looking for a loft because that don't cost no whole lot of bread, you know, and that way I can work without Tish being bugged to death. This room ain't big enough for one, ain't no question about its being big enough for two, and I got all my work here, and in the basement." He is rolling a cigarette as he says this, for him and for Daniel, squatting opposite him. "They got lofts standing empty all over the East Side, man, and don't nobody want to rent them, except freaks like me. And they all fire traps and some of them ain't even got no toilets. So, you figure like finding a loft ain't going to be no sweat." He lights the cigarette, takes a drag, and hands it to Daniel. "But, man—this country really do not like niggers. They do not like niggers so bad, man, they will rent to a leper first. I swear." Daniel drags on the cigarette, hands it back to Fonny—*Tired old ladies kissing dogs!* cries the record player—who drags on it, takes a sip of his beer and hands it back. "Sometimes Tish and I go together, sometimes she goes alone, sometimes I go alone. But it's always the same story, man." He stands up. "And now I can't let Tish go alone no more because, dig, last week we thought we *had* us a loft, the cat had promised it to her. But he had not seen *me*. And he figures a black chick by herself, way downtown, looking for a loft, well, he *know* he going to make it with *her*. *He* thinks she's propositioning him, that's what he *really* thinks. And Tish comes to tell me, just so proud and happy"—he sits down again—"and we go on over there. And when the cat sees me, he says there's been some great misunderstanding, he *can't* rent the loft because he's got all these relatives coming in from Rumania like in half an hour and he got to give it to *them*. Shit. And I *told* him he was full of shit and he threatened to call the cops on my ass." He takes the cigarette from Daniel. "I'm really going to have to try to figure out some way of getting some bread together and getting out of this fucking country."

"How you going to do that?"

"I don't know yet," says Fonny. "Tish can't swim." He gives the cigarette back to Daniel, and they whoop and rock with laughter.

"Maybe you could go first," says Daniel, soberly.

The cigarette and the record are finished.

"No," says Fonny, "I don't think I want to do that." Daniel watches him. "I'd be too scared."

"Scared of what?" asks Daniel—though he really knows the answer to this question.

"Just scared," says Fonny—after a long silence.

"Scared of what might happen to Tish?" Daniel asks.

There is another long silence. Fonny is staring out the window. Daniel is staring at Fonny's back.

"Yes," Fonny says, finally. Then, "Scared of what might happen to both of us—without each other. Like Tish ain't got no sense at all, man—she trusts everybody. She walk down the street, swinging that little behind of hers, and she's *surprised*, man, when some cat tries to jump her. She don't see what I see." And silence falls again, Daniel watching him, and Fonny says, "I know I might seem to be a weird kind of cat. But I got two things in my life, man—I got my wood and stone and I got Tish. If I lose them, I'm lost. I know that. You know"—and now he turns to face Daniel—"whatever's in me I didn't put there. And I can't take it out."

Daniel moves to the pallet, leans against the wall. "I don't know if you so *weird*. I know you lucky. I ain't got nothing like that. Can I have another beer, man?"

"Sure," Fonny says, and goes to open two more cans. He hands one to Daniel and Daniel takes a long swallow before he says, "I just come out the slammer, baby. Two years."

Fonny says nothing—just turns and looks.

Daniel says nothing; swallows a little more beer.

"They said—they still *say*—stole a car. Man, I can't even *drive* a car, and I tried to make my lawyer—but he was really *their* lawyer, dig, he worked for the city—prove that, but he didn't. And, anyway, I wasn't in no car when they picked me up. But I had a little grass on me. I was on my stoop. And so they come and picked me up, like that, you know, it was about midnight, and they locked me up and then the next morning they put me in the lineup and somebody said it was *me* stole the car—that car I ain't seen yet. And so—you know—since I had that weed on me, they had me anyhow and so they said if I would plead guilty they'd give me a lighter sentence. If I *didn't* plead guilty, they'd throw me the book. Well"—he sips his beer again—"I was alone, baby, wasn't nobody, and so I entered the guilty plea. Two years!" He leans forward, staring at Fonny. "But, then, it sounded a whole lot better than the marijuana charge." He leans back and laughs and sips his beer and looks up at Fonny. "It wasn't. I let them fuck over me because I was scared and dumb and I'm sorry now." He is silent. Then, "Two years!"

"By the balls," says Fonny.

"Yes," says Daniel—after the loudest and longest silence either of them has ever known.

When I come back in, they are both sitting there, a little high, and I say nothing and I move about in the tiny space of the kitchenette as quietly as I can. Fonny comes in for a moment and rubs up against me from behind and hugs me and kisses the nape of my neck. Then, he returns to Daniel.

"How long you been out?"

"About three months." He leaves the pallet, walks to the window. "Man, it was bad. Very bad. And it's bad now. Maybe I'd feel different if I had done something and got caught. But I didn't do nothing. They were just playing with me, man, because they could. And I'm lucky it was only two years, you dig? Because they can do with you whatever they want. *Whatever they want.* And they dogs, man. I really found out, in the slammer, what Malcolm and them cats was talking about. The white man's *got* to be the devil. He sure ain't a man. Some of the things I saw, baby, I'll be dreaming about until the day I die."

Fonny puts one hand on Daniel's neck. Daniel shudders. Tears stream down his face.

"I know," Fonny says, gently, "but try not to let it get to you too tough. You out now, it's over, you young."

"Man, I know what you're saying. And I appreciate

it. But you don't know—the worst thing, man, the *worst* thing—is that they can make you so fucking *scared.* Scared, man. *Scared.*"

Fonny says nothing, simply stands there, with his hand on Daniel's neck.

I yell, from the kitchen, "You cats hungry?"

"Yeah," Fonny yells back, "we starving. *Move* it!"

Daniel dries his eyes and comes to the door of the kitchenette and smiles at me.

"It's nice to see you, Tish. You sure ain't gained no weight, have you?"

"You hush. I'm skinny because I'm *poor.*"

"Well, I sure don't know why you didn't pick yourself a rich husband. You ain't *never* going to gain no weight *now.*"

"Well, if you skinny, Daniel, you can move faster and when you in a tight place, you got a better chance of getting out of it. You see what I mean."

"You sound like you got it figured. You learn all that from Fonny?"

"I learned *some* things from Fonny. But I also have a swift, natural intelligence—haven't you been struck by it?"

"Tish, I been struck by so many things that I really have not had time to do you justice."

"You're not the only one. And I can't really blame you. I'm so remarkable, I sometimes have to pinch myself."

Daniel laughs. "I'd like to see that. Where?"

Fonny mutters, "She's so remarkable, I sometimes have to go up side her head."

"He beats you, too?"

"Ah! what *can* I do—? *All my life is just despair, but I don't care*—"

Suddenly we are singing,

> *When he takes me in his arms,*
> *The world is bright, all right.*
> *What's the difference if I say*
> *I'll go away*
> *When I know I'll come back*
> *On my knees someday*
> *For, whatever my man is*
> *I am his,*
> *Forevermore!*

Then, we are laughing. Daniel sobers, looking within, suddenly very far away. "Poor Billie," he says, "they beat the living crap out of *her*, too."

"Man," Fonny says, "we just have to move it from day to day. If you think too much about it, you really *are* fucked, can't move at all."

"Let's eat," I say. "Come on."

I have prepared what I know Fonny likes: ribs and cornbread and rice, with gravy, and green peas. Fonny puts on the record player, low: Marvin Gaye's "What's Going On."

"Maybe Tish can't gain no weight," says Daniel, after a moment, "but *you* sure will. You folks mind if I drop by more often—say, around this time?"

"Feel free," says Fonny, cheerfully, and winks at me. "Tish ain't very good looking, but she can sure get the pots together."

"I'm happy to know I have some human use," I tell him, and he winks at me again, and starts chewing on a rib.

Fonny: chews on the rib, and watches me: and, in complete silence, without moving a muscle, we are laughing with each other. We are laughing for many reasons. We are together somewhere where no one can reach us, touch us, joined. We are happy, even, that we have food enough for Daniel, who eats peacefully, not knowing that we are laughing, but sensing that something wonderful has happened to us, which means that wonderful things happen, and that maybe something wonderful will happen to *him*. It's wonderful, anyway, to be able to help a person to have that feeling.

Daniel stays with us till midnight. He's a little afraid to leave, afraid, in fact, to hit those streets, and Fonny realizes this and walks him to the subway. Daniel, who cannot abandon his mother, yet longs to be free to confront his life; is terrified at the same time of what that life may bring, is terrified of freedom; and is struggling in a trap. And Fonny, who is younger, struggles now to be older, in order to help his friend toward his deliverance. *Didn't my Lord deliver Daniel? And why not every man?*

The song is old, the question unanswered.

On their walk that night, and many nights thereafter, Daniel tried to tell Fonny something about what had happened to him, in prison. Sometimes he was at the house, and so I heard it, too; sometimes, he and Fonny were alone. Sometimes, when Daniel spoke, he cried—sometimes, Fonny held him. Sometimes, I did. Daniel brought it out, or forced it out, or tore it out of himself as though it were torn, twisted, chilling metal, bringing with it his flesh and his blood—he tore it out of himself like a man trying to be cured:

"You don't know what's happening to you, at first. No way to know it. They come and got me off my stoop and they searched me. When I thought about it later, I realized that I didn't really know *why*. I was always on that stoop, me and the other cats, and they was always passing by, and, while *I* wasn't never on no shit, they knew some of the other cats has to be—you *know* they knew it. And they could see the dudes scratching and nodding. I think they dug that. When I thought about it later, I thought to myself, the motherfuckers really dig that shit. They go on into headquarters and report, Everything's cool, sir. We escorted the French connection while he made his rounds and the shit's been delivered and the niggers is out of it. But this night I was by myself, about to go on in, and they stopped the car and yelled at me and pushed me into the hallway and searched me. *You* know how they do it."

I *don't* know. But Fonny nods, his face still, his eyes very dark.

"And I had just picked up this grass, it was in my

: 115 :

ass-pocket. And so they pulled it out, man, do they *love* to pat your ass, and one of them give it to the other and one of them handcuffed me and pushed me into the car. And I hadn't known it was going to come to that, maybe I was a little high, maybe I hadn't had time to think, but, baby, when that man put his handcuffs on me and pushed me down the steps and on into the car and then that car started moving, I wanted to scream for my Mama. And then I started getting scared, because she can't hardly do nothing for herself, and she'd start to worrying about me, and wouldn't nobody know where I was! They took me down to the precinct and they booked me on a narcotics charge and they took everything I had off of me and I started to ask, Can I make a phone call? and then I realized that I didn't really have nobody to call, except my Mama, and who *she* going to call this hour of night? I just hoped she was sleeping, you know, like she had just figured that I was out late, and, by time she woke up in the morning and realized I wasn't there that maybe I'd have figured out—something. They put me in this little cell with about four or five other cats, they was just nodding and farting, and I sat there and I tried to get my mind together. Because what the fuck am I going to do? I ain't got nobody to call—I really *don't*, except maybe that Jew I work for; he a nice enough dude, but, man, he ain't hardly going to dig it. What I'm really trying to figure is how I can get somebody *else* to call my Mama, somebody who's cool, who can cool *her*, somebody who can *do* something. But I can't think of nobody.

"Morning came and they put us in the wagon. There's this old white motherfucker they picked up off the Bowery—I guess—he done vomited all over himself and he's looking down at the floor and he's singing. He can't sing, but he sure is stinking. And, man, I'm sure grateful I ain't on no shit because now one of the brothers is started to moan, he got his arms wrapped around himself, and sweat is starting to pour off that cat, like water down a scrubbing board. I ain't much older than he is, and I sure wish I could help him but I know I can't do nothing. And I think to myself, Now, the cops who put him in this wagon know that this dude is *sick*. I *know* they know it. He ain't supposed to be in here—and him not hardly much more than a kid. But the mothers who put him in this wagon, man, they was coming in their pants while they did it. I don't believe there's a white man in this country, baby, who can even *get* his dick hard, without he hear some nigger moan.

"Well, we get on down there. And I still ain't thought of nobody to call. I want to shit and I want to die, but I know I can't do neither. I figure they'll let me shit when they get ready, in the meantime I just got to hold it best I can, and it just pure foolishness for me to think of wanting to die because they can kill me any time they want to and maybe I'll die today. Before I shit. And then I think of my Mama again. I *know* she worried by now."

Sometimes Fonny held him, sometimes I did. Sometimes, he stood at the window, with his back to us.

"I can't really tell you much more about it—maybe theres' a whole lot of shit that I won't never be *able* to tell nobody. They had me on the grass, and so they nailed me on the car—that car I ain't seen yet. I guess they just happened to need a car thief that day. Sure wish I knew whose car it was. I hope it wasn't no black dude's car, though."

Then, sometimes, Daniel would grin, sometimes he would dry his eyes. We would eat and drink together. Daniel was trying very hard to get past something, something unnamable: he was trying as hard as a man can try. And sometimes I held him, sometimes Fonny: we were all he had.

On the Tuesday after the Monday that I saw Hayward, I saw Fonny at the six o'clock visit. I had never seen him so upset before.

"What the fuck we going to do about Mrs. Rogers? Where the fuck did she go?"

"I don't know. But we'll find her."

"*How* you going to find her?"

"We're sending people to Puerto Rico. We think that's where she went."

"And suppose she went to Argentina? or Chile? or China?"

"Fonny. Please. How's she going to get that far?"

"They can give her the money, to go anywhere!"

"Who?"

"The D.A.'s office, that's who!"

"Fonny——"

"You don't believe me? You don't think they can do it?"

"I don't think they have."

"How you going to get the money to find her?"

"We're all working, all of us."

"Yeah. My Daddy's working in the garment center, you're working in a department store, *your* Daddy's working on the waterfront——!"

"Fonny. Listen——"

"Listen to what? What we going to do about that fucking lawyer? He don't give a shit about me, he don't give a shit about *nobody!* You want me to die in here? You know what's going on in here? You know what's happening to me, to *me, to me,* in *here?*"

"Fonny. Fonny. Fonny."

"I'm sorry, baby. I don't mean none of that for you. I'm sorry. I love you, Tish. I'm sorry."

"I love you, Fonny. I love you."

"How's the baby coming?"

"It's growing. It'll start showing more next month."

We stared at each other.

"Get me out of here, baby. Get me out of here. Please."

"I promise. I promise. I promise."

"Don't cry. I'm sorry I yelled. I wasn't yelling at you, Tish."

"I know."

"Please don't cry. Please don't cry. It's bad for the baby."

"All right."

"Give us a smile, Tish."

"Is that all right?"

"You can do better than that."

"Is this better?"

"Yeah. Give us a kiss."

I kissed the glass. He kissed the glass.

"You still love me?"

"I'll always love you, Fonny."

"I love you. I miss you. I miss everything about you, I miss everything we had together, everything we did together, walking and talking and making love—oh, baby, get me out of here."

"I will. Hold on."

"I promise.—Later."

"Later."

He followed the guard into the unimaginable inferno, and I stood up, my knees and elbows shaking, to cross the Sahara again.

That night I dreamed, I dreamed all night, I had terrible dreams. In one of these dreams, Fonny was driving a truck, a great big truck, very fast, too fast, down the highway, and he was looking for me. But he didn't see me. I was behind the truck, calling out his name, but the roar of the motor drowned my voice. There were two turnings off this highway, and they both looked exactly alike. The highway was on a cliff, above the sea. One of the turnings led to the driveway of our house; the other led to the cliff's edge and a drop straight down to the sea. He was driving too fast, too fast! I called his name as loud as I could and, as he began to turn the truck, I screamed again and woke up.

The light was on, and Sharon was standing above me. I cannot describe her face. She had brought in a cold, wet towel and she wiped my brow and my neck. She leaned down and kissed me.

Then, she straightened and looked into my eyes.

"I know I can't help you very much right now—God knows what I wouldn't give if I could. But I know about suffering; if that helps. I know that it ends. I ain't going to tell you no lies, like it always ends for the better. Sometimes it ends for the worse. You can suffer so bad that you can be driven to a place where you can't ever suffer again: and that's worse."

She took both my hands and held them tightly between her own. "Try to remember that. And: the only way *anything* ever gets done is when you make up your mind to do it. I know a lot of our loved ones, a lot of our men, have died in prison: but not *all* of them. You remember that. And: you ain't really alone in that bed, Tish. You got that child beneath your heart and we're all counting on you, Fonny's counting on *you*, to bring that child here safe and well. You the only one who can do it. But you're strong. Lean on your strength."

I said, "Yes. Yes, Mama." I knew I didn't have any strength. But I was going to have to find some, somewhere.

"Are you all right now? Can you sleep?"

"Yes."

"I don't want to sound foolish. But, just remember, love brought you here. If you trusted love this far, don't panic now."

And, again, she kissed me and she turned out the light and she left me.

I lay there—wide awake; and very frightened. *Get me out of here.*

I remembered women I had known, but scarcely looked at, who had frightened me; because they knew how to use their bodies in order to get something that they wanted. I now began to realize that my judgment of these women had had very little to do with morals. (And I now began to wonder about the meaning of this word.) My judgment had been due to my sense of how little they appeared to want. I could not conceive of peddling myself for so low a price.

But, for a higher price? for Fonny?

And I fell asleep; for a while; and then I woke up. I had never been so tired in my life. I ached all over. I looked at the clock and I realized that it would soon be time to get up and go to work, unless I called in sick. But I could not call in sick.

I got dressed and went out to the kitchen, to have tea with Mama. Joseph and Ernestine had already gone. Mama and I sipped our tea in almost total silence. Something was turning over and over and over, in my mind: I could not speak.

I came down into the streets. It was a little past eight o'clock. I walked these morning streets; these streets are never empty. I passed the old blind black man on the corner. Perhaps I had seen him all my life. But I wondered about his life, for the first time, now. There were about four kids, all junkies, standing on the corner, talking. Some women were rushing to work. I tried to read their faces. Some women were finally going to get a little rest, and they headed off the avenue, to their furnished rooms. Every side street was piled high with garbage, and garbage was piled high before every stoop along the avenue. I thought, If I'm going to peddle ass, I better not try it up here. It would take just as long as scrubbing floors, and be a lot more painful. What I was really thinking was, I know I can't do it before the baby comes, but, if Fonny's not out by then, maybe I'll have to try it. Maybe I better get ready. But there was something else turning over, at the bottom of my mind, which I knew I didn't have the courage to look at yet.

Get ready, how? I walked down the steps and pushed through the turnstile and stood on the subway platform, with the others. When the train came, I pushed in, with the others, and I leaned against a pole, while their breath and smell rolled over me. Cold sweat covered my forehead and began to trickle down my armpits and my back. I hadn't thought of it before, because I knew I had to keep on working up to just about the last minute; but now I began to wonder just how, as I became heavier and sicker, I was going to get to work. If I should pass out, these people, getting on and getting off, would simply trample me and the baby to death. *We're counting on you—Fonny's counting on you—Fonny's counting on you, to bring that baby here, safe and well.* I held the white bar more firmly. My freezing body shook.

I looked around the subway car. It was a little like the

drawings I had seen of slave ships. Of course, they hadn't had newspapers on the slave ships, hadn't needed them yet; but, as concerned space (and also, perhaps, as concerned intention) the principle was exactly the same. A heavy man, smelling of hot sauce and toothpaste, breathed heavily into my face. It wasn't his fault that he had to breathe, or that my face was there. His body pressed against me, too, very hard, but this did not mean that he was thinking of rape, or thinking of me at all. He was probably wondering only—and that, dimly—how he was going to get through another day on his job. And he certainly did not see me.

And, when a subway car is packed—unless it's full of people who know each other, going on a picnic, say—it is almost always silent. It's as though everybody is just holding his breath, waiting to get out of there. Each time the train comes into a station, and some of the people push you aside, in order to get out—as happened now, for example, with the man who smelled of hot sauce and toothpaste—a great sigh seems to rise; stifled immediately by the people who get on. Now, a blond girl, carrying a bandbox, was breathing her hangover into my face. My stop came, and I got off, climbed the steps and crossed the street. I went into the service entrance and punched the clock, put my street clothes away and went out to my counter. I was a little late for the floor, but I'd clocked in on time.

The floor manager, a white boy, young, nice enough, gave me a mock scowl as I hurried to my place.

It isn't only old white ladies who come to that counter

to smell the back of my hand. Very rarely does a black cat come anywhere near this counter, and if, or when, he does, his intentions are often more generous and always more precise. Perhaps, for a black cat, I really do, too closely, resemble a helpless baby sister. He doesn't want to see me turn into a whore. And perhaps some black cats come closer, just to look into my eyes, just to hear my voice, to check out what's happening. And they never smell the back of my hand: a black cat puts out *his* hand, and you spray it, and he carries the back of his own hand to his own nostrils. And he doesn't bother to pretend that he's come to buy perfume. Sometimes, he does—buy some perfume; most often he doesn't. Sometimes the hand he has brought down from his nostrils clenches itself into a secret fist, and, with that prayer, that salutation, he moves away. But a white man will carry your hand to his nostrils, he will hold it there. I watched everybody, all day long, with something turning over and over and over, in my mind. Ernestine came to pick me up at the end of the day. She said that Mrs. Rogers had been located, in Santurce, Puerto Rico; and someone of us would have to go there.

"With Hayward?"

"No. Hayward's got to deal with Bell, and the D.A. here. Anyway, you can see that, for many, many reasons, Hayward *can't* go. He'd be accused of intimidating a witness."

"But that's what *they're* doing—!"

"Tish"—we were walking up Eighth Avenue, toward

Columbus Circle—"it would take us until your baby is voting age to prove *that*."

"Are we going to take the subway, or the bus?"

"We're going to sit down somewhere until this rush hour's over. You and me, we've got to talk anyway, before we talk to Mama and Daddy. They don't know yet. I haven't talked to them yet."

And I realize how much Ernestine loves me, at the same time that I remember that she is, after all, only four years older than I.

Mrs. Victoria Rogers, née Victoria Maria San Felipe Sanchez, declares that on the evening of March 5, between the hours of eleven and twelve, in the vestibule of her home, she was criminally assaulted by a man she now knows to have been Alonzo Hunt, and was used by the aforesaid Hunt in the most extreme and abominable sexual manner, and forced to undergo the most unimaginable sexual perversions.

I have never seen her. I know only that an American-born Irishman, Gary Rogers, an engineer, went to Puerto Rico about six years ago, and there met Victoria, who was then about eighteen. He married her, and brought her to the mainland. His career did not go up, but down; he seems to have become embittered. In any case, having pumped three children out of her, he left. I know nothing about the man with whom she was living on Orchard Street, with whom, presumably, she had fled to Puerto Rico. The children are, presumably, somewhere on the mainland, with her relatives. Her "home" is Orchard Street. She lived on the fourth floor. If the rape took place in the "vestibule," then she was raped on the ground floor, under the staircase. It could have taken place on the fourth floor, but it seems unlikely; there are four apartments on that floor. Orchard Street, if you know New York, is a very long way from Bank Street. Orchard Street is damn near in the East River and Bank Street is practically in the Hudson. It is not possible to run from Orchard to Bank, particularly not with the police behind you. Yet, Bell *swears* that he saw Fonny "run from the scene of the crime." This is possible only if Bell were off duty, for his "beat" is on the West Side, not the East. Yet, Bell could arrest Fonny out of the house on Bank Street. It is then up to the accused to prove, and pay for proving, the irregularity and improbability of this sequence of events.

Ernestine and I had sat down in the last booth of a bar off Columbus.

Ernestine's way with me, and with all her children, is to drop something heavy on you and then lean back, calculating how you'll take it. She's got to know that, in order to calculate her own position: the net's got to be in place.

Now, maybe because I had spent so much of the day, and the night before, with my terrors—and my calculations—concerning the possible sale of my body, I began to see the reality of rape.

I asked, "Do you think she really was raped?"

"Tish. I don't know what's going on in that busy, ingrown mind of yours, but that question has no bearing on anything. As far as our situation is concerned, baby, she was raped. That's it." She paused and sipped her drink. She sounded very calm, but her forehead was tense, intelligent, with terror. "I think, in fact, that she was raped and that she has absolutely no idea who did it, would probably not even recognize him if he passed her on the street. I may sound crazy, but the mind works that way. She'd recognize him if he raped her *again*. But then it would no longer be rape. If you see what I mean."

"I see what you mean. But why does she accuse Fonny?"

"Because Fonny was presented to her as the rapist and it was much easier to say yes than to try and relive the whole damn thing again. This way, it's over, for her. Except for the trial. But, then, it's really over. For her."

"And for us, too?"

"No." She looked at me very steadily. It may seem a funny thing to say, but I found myself admiring her guts. "It won't be over for us." She spoke very carefully, watching me all the while. "There's a way in which it may never be over, for us. But we won't talk about that now. Listen. We have to think about it very seriously, and in another way. That's why I wanted to have a drink alone with you, before we went home."

"What are you trying to tell me?" I was suddenly very frightened.

"Listen. I don't think that we can get her to change her testimony. You've got to understand: she's not lying."

"What are you trying to tell me? What the fuck do you mean, she's not lying?"

"Will you listen to me? Please? Of course, she's *lying*. *We* know she's lying. But—*she's*—not—*lying*. As far as she's concerned, Fonny raped her and that's that, and now she hasn't got to deal with it anymore. It's over. For her. If she changes her testimony, she'll go mad. Or become another woman. And you know how often people go mad, and how rarely they change."

"So—what are we to do?"

"We have to disprove the state's case. There's no point in saying that we have to make *them* prove it, because, as far as they're concerned, the accusation *is* the proof and that's exactly the way those nuts in the jury box will take it, quiet as it's kept. *They're* liars, too—and *we* know they're liars. But *they* don't."

I remembered, for some reason, something someone had said to me, a long time ago—it might have been Fonny: *A fool never says he's a fool.*

"We can't disprove it. Daniel's in jail."

"Yes. But Hayward is seeing him tomorrow."

"That don't mean nothing. Daniel is still going to change his testimony, I bet you."

"He may. He may not. But I have another idea."

There we sat, in this dirty bar, two sisters, trying to be cool.

"Let's say the worst comes to the worst. Mrs. Rogers

will not change her testimony. Let's say Daniel changes his. That leaves only Officer Bell, doesn't it?"

"Yes. And so what?"

"Well—I have a file on him. A long file. I can prove that he murdered a twelve-year-old black boy, in Brooklyn, two years ago. That's how come he was transferred to Manhattan. I know the mother of the murdered boy. And I know Bell's wife, who hates him."

"She can't testify against him."

"She hasn't got to testify against him. She just has to sit in that courtroom, and watch him—"

"I don't see how this helps us—at all——"

"I know you don't. And you may be right. But, if worse comes to worst, and it's always better to assume that it will—come to worst—then our tactic has to be to shatter the credibility of the state's only witness."

"Ernestine," I said, "you're dreaming."

"I don't think I am. I'm gambling. If I can get those two women, one white and one black, to sit in that courtroom, and if Hayward does his work right, we ought to be able to shatter the case, on cross-examination. Remember, Tish, that, after all, it isn't very much of a case. If Fonny were white, it wouldn't be a case at all."

Well. I understand what she means. I know where she's coming from. It's a long shot. But, in our position, after all, only the long shot counts. We don't have any other: that's it. And I realize, too, that if we thought it were feasible, we might very well be sitting here, cool, very cool, discussing ways and means of having Bell's head blown off. And, when it was done, we'd shrug and have another drink: that's it. People don't know.

"Yes. Okay. What about Puerto Rico?"

"That's one of the reasons I wanted to talk to you. Before we talk to Mama and Daddy. Look. *You* can't go. You've got to be here. For one thing, without you, Fonny will panic. I don't see how *I* can go. I've got to keep lighting firecrackers under Hayward's ass. Obviously, a man can't go. Daddy can't go, and God knows Frank can't go. That leaves—Mama."

"Mama—?"

"Yes."

"She don't want to go to Puerto Rico."

"That's right. And she hates planes. But she wants your baby's father out of jail. Of course she doesn't want to go to Puerto Rico. But she'll go."

"And what do you think she can *do?*"

"She can do something no special investigator can do. She may be able to break through to Mrs. Rogers. Maybe not—but if she can, we're ahead. And if not—well, we haven't lost anything, and, at least, we'll know we've tried."

I watch her forehead. Okay.

"And what about Daniel?"

"I told you. Hayward is seeing him tomorrow. He *may* have been able to see him today. He's calling us tonight."

I lean back. "Some shit."

"Yeah. But we in it now."

Then, we are silent. I realize, for the first time, that

the bar is loud. And I look around me. It's actually a terrible place and I realize that the people here can only suppose that Ernestine and I are tired whores, or a Lesbian couple, or both. Well. We are certainly in it now, and it may get worse. It will, certainly—and now something almost as hard to catch as a whisper in a crowded place, as light and as definite as a spider's web, strikes below my ribs, stunning and astonishing my heart—get worse. But that light tap, that kick, that signal, announces to me that what can get worse can get better. Yes. It will get worse. But the baby, turning for the first time in its incredible veil of water, announces its presence and claims me; tells me, in that instant, that what can get worse can get better; and that what can get better can get worse. In the meantime—forever— it is entirely up to me. The baby cannot get here without me. And, while I may have known this, in one way, a little while ago, now the baby knows it, and tells me that while it will certainly be worse, once it leaves the water, what gets worse can also get better. It will be in the water for a while yet: but it is preparing itself for a transformation. And so must I.

I said, "It's all right. I'm not afraid."

And Ernestine smiled, and said, "Let's move it then."

Joseph and Frank, as we learn later, have also been sitting in a bar, and this is what happened between them:

Joseph has a certain advantage over Frank—though it is only now that he begins to realize, or, rather, suspect it—in that he has no sons. He has always wanted a son; this fact cost Ernestine far more than it cost me; for, by the time I came along, he was reconciled. If he had had sons, they might very well be dead, or in jail. And they both know, facing each other in the booth of a bar on Lenox Avenue, that it is a miracle that Joseph's daughters are not on the block. Both of them know far more than either of them would like to know, and certainly far more than either can say, concerning the disasters which have overtaken the women in Frank's house.

And Frank looks down, holding his drink tightly between both hands: *he* has a son. And Joseph sips his beer and watches him. That son is also *his* son now, and that makes Frank his brother.

They are both grown men, approaching fifty, and they are both in terrible trouble.

Neither of them look it. Joseph is much darker than Frank, black, deep-set, hooded eyes, stern, still, a high forehead in which one vein beats, leftward, a forehead so high that it can make you think of cathedrals. His lips are always a little twisted. Only those who know him—only those who love him—know when this twist signals laughter, love, or fury. The key is to be found in the pulsing vein in the forehead. The lips change very little, the eyes change all the time: and when Joseph is happy, and when he laughs, something absolutely miraculous is happening. He then looks, I swear to you,—and his hair is beginning to turn gray,—about thirteen years old. I thought once, I'm certainly glad I didn't meet him when he was a young man and then I thought, But you're his daughter, and then I dropped into a paralyzed silence, thinking: Wow.

Frank is light, thinner. I don't think that you can describe my father as handsome; but you can describe Frank that way. I don't mean to be putting him down when I say that because that face has paid, and is paying, a dreadful price. People make you pay for the way you look, which is also the way *you* think you look, and what time writes in a human face is the record of that collision. Frank has survived it, barely. His forehead is lined like the palm of a hand—unreadable; his graying hair is thick and curls violently upward from the widow's peak. His lips are not as thick as Joseph's and do not dance that way, are pressed tightly together, as though he wished they would disappear. His cheekbones are high, and his large dark eyes slant upward, like Fonny's—Fonny has his father's eyes.

Joseph certainly cannot realize this in the way that his daughter knows it. But he stares at Frank in silence, and forces Frank to raise his eyes.

"What we going to do?" Frank asks.

"Well, the first thing we got to do," says Joseph, resolutely, "is to stop blaming each other, and stop blaming ourselves. If we can't do that, man, we'll never get the boy out because *we'll* be so fucked up. And we cannot fuck up now, baby, and I know you hear where I'm coming from."

"Man, what," asks Frank—with his little smile—"we going to do about the money?"

"You ever have any money?" Joseph asks.

Frank looks up at him and says nothing—merely questions him with his eyes.

Joseph asks again, "You ever have any money?"

Frank says, finally, "No."

"Then, why you worried about it now?"

Frank looks up at him again.

"You raised them somehow, didn't you? You fed them somehow—didn't you? If we start to worrying about money now, man, we going to be fucked and we going to lose our children. That white man, baby, and may his balls shrivel and his ass-hole rot, he *want* you to be worried about the money. That's his whole game. But if we got to where we are without money, we can get further. I ain't worried about they money—they ain't got no right to it anyhow, they stole it from us—they ain't never met nobody they didn't lie to and steal from. Well, I can steal, too. *And* rob. How you think I raised my daughters? Shit."

But Frank is not Joseph. He stares down again, into his drink.

"What you think is going to happen?"

"What we *make* happen," says Joseph—again, with resolution.

"That's easy to say," says Frank.

"Not if you mean it," says Joseph.

There is a long silence into which neither man speaks. Even the jukebox is silent.

"I guess," Frank says, finally, "I love Fonny more than I love anybody in this world. And it makes me ashamed, man, I swear, because he was a real sweet manly little boy, wasn't scared of nothing—except maybe his Mama. He didn't understand his Mama." Frank stops. "And I don't know what I should have done. I ain't a woman. And there's some things only a woman can do with a child. And I thought she loved him—like I guess I thought, one time, she loved me." Frank sips his drink, and he tries to smile. "I don't know if I was ever any kind of father to him—any kind of *real* father—and now he's in jail and it ain't his fault and I don't even know how I'm going to get him out. I'm sure one hell of a man."

"Well," says Joseph, "*he* sure think you are. He loves you, and he respects you—now, you got to remember that *I* might know that much better than you. Tell you something else. Your baby son is the father of my baby daughter's baby. Now, how you going to sit here and act like can't nothing be done? We got a child on the way here, man. You want me to beat the shit out of you?" He says this with ferocity; but, after a moment, he smiles. "I know," he says, then, carefully, "I know. But I know some hustles and you know some hustles and these are our children and we got to set them free." Joseph finishes his beer. "So, let's drink up, man, and go on in. We got a whole lot of shit to deal with, in a hurry."

Frank finishes his drink, and straightens his shoulders. "You right, old buddy. Let's make it."

The date for Fonny's trial keeps changing. This fact, paradoxically, forces me to realize that Hayward's concern is genuine. I don't think that he very much cared, in the beginning. He had never taken a case like Fonny's before, and it was Ernestine, acting partly out of experience but mainly out of instinct, who had bludgeoned him into it. But, once into it, the odor of shit rose high; and he had no choice but to keep on stirring it. It became obvious at once, for example, that the degree of his concern for his client—or the fact that he had any genuine concern for his client at all—placed him at odds, at loggerheads, with the keepers of the keys and seals. He had not expected this, and at first it bewildered, then frightened, then angered him. He swiftly understood that he was between the carrot and the stick: he couldn't avoid the stick but he had to make it clear, finally, that he'd be damned if he'd go for the carrot. This had the effect of isolating, indeed of branding him, and, as this increased Fonny's danger, it also increased Hayward's responsibility. It did not help that I distrusted him, Ernestine harangued him, Mama was laconic, and, for Joseph, he was just another white boy with a college degree.

Although, naturally, in the beginning, I distrusted him, I am not really what you can call a distrustful person: and, anyway, as time wore on, with each of us trying to hide our terror from the other, we began to depend more and more on one another—we had no choice. And I began to see, as time wore on, that, for Hayward, the battle increasingly became a private one, involving neither gratitude nor public honor. It was a sordid, a banal case, this rape by a black boy of an ignorant Puerto Rican woman—what was he getting so excited about? And so his colleagues scorned and avoided him. This fact introduced yet other dangers, not least of them the danger of retreating into the self-pitying and quixotic. But Fonny was too real a presence, and Hayward too proud a man for that.

But the calendars were full—it would take about a thousand years to try all the people in the American prisons, but the Americans are optimistic and still hope for time—and sympathetic or merely intelligent judges are as rare as snowstorms in the tropics. There was the obscene power and the ferocious enmity of the D.A.'s office. Thus, Hayward walked a chalk line, maneuvering very hard to bring Fonny before a judge who would really listen to the case. For this, Hayward needed charm, patience, money, and a backbone of tempered steel.

He managed to see Daniel, who has been beaten. He cannot arrange for his release because Daniel has been booked on a narcotics charge. Without becoming Daniel's lawyer, he cannot visit him. He suggests this to Daniel, but Daniel is evasive and afraid. Hayward suspects that Daniel has also been drugged and he does not know if he dares bring Daniel to the witness stand, or not.

So. There we are. Mama begins letting out my clothes, and I go to work wearing jackets and slacks. But it's clear that I'm not going to be able to keep working much longer: I've got to be able to visit Fonny every instant that I can. Joseph is working overtime, double time, and so is Frank. Ernestine has to spend less time with her children because she has taken a job as part-time private secretary to a very rich and eccentric young actress, whose connections she intends to intimidate, and use. Joseph is coldly, systematically, stealing from the docks, and Frank is stealing from the garment center and they sell the hot goods in Harlem, or in Brooklyn. They don't tell us this, but we know it. They don't tell us because, if things go wrong, we can't be accused of being accomplices. We cannot penetrate their silence, we must not try. Each of these men would gladly go to jail, blow away a pig, or blow up a city, to save their progeny from the jaws of this democratic hell.

Now, Sharon must begin preparing for her Puerto Rican journey, and Hayward briefs her:

"She is not actually in Santurce, but a little beyond it, in what might once have been called a suburb, but which is now far worse than what we would call a slum. In Puerto Rico, I believe it is called a *favella*. I have been to Puerto Rico once, and so I will not try to describe a *favella*. And I am sure, when you return, that you will not try to describe it, either."

Hayward looks at her, at once distant and intense, and hands her a typewritten sheet of paper. "This is the address. But I think that you will understand, almost as soon as you get where you are going, that the word 'address' has almost no meaning—it would be more honest to say: this is the neighborhood."

Sharon, wearing her floppy beige beret, looks at it.

"There's no phone," says Hayward, "and, anyway, a phone is the very last thing you need. You might as well send up flares. But it isn't hard to find. Just follow your nose."

They stare at each other.

"Now," says Hayward, with his really painful smile, "just to make things easier for you, I must tell you that we are not really certain under which name she is living. Her maiden name is Sanchez—but that's a little like looking for a Mrs. Jones or a Mr. Smith. Her married name is Rogers; but I am sure that that appears only on her passport. The name of what we must call her common-law husband"—and now he pauses to look down at another sheet of paper, and then at Sharon and then at me—"is Pietro Thomasino Alvarez."

He hands Sharon this piece of paper; and, again, Sharon studies it.

"And," says Hayward, "take this with you. I hope it will help. She still looks this way. It was snapped last week."

And he hands Sharon a photograph, slightly larger than passport size.

I have never seen her. I stand, to peer over Sharon's shoulder. She is blond—but are Puerto Ricans blond? She is smiling up into the camera a constipated smile; yet, there is life in the eyes. The eyes and the eyebrows are dark, and the dark shoulders are bare.

"This from a night club?" Sharon asks; and, "Yes," Hayward answers, she watching him, he watching her: and:

"Does she work there?" Sharon asks.

"No," says Hayward. "But Pietro does."

I keep studying, over my mother's shoulder, the face of my most mortal enemy.

Mama turns the photograph over, and holds it in her lap.

"And how old is this Pietro?"

"About—twenty-two," says Hayward.

And just exactly like, as the song puts it, *God arose! In a windstorm! And he troubled everybody's mind!* silence fell in the office. Mama leans forward, thinking ahead.

"Twenty-two," she says, slowly.

"Yes," says Hayward. "I'm afraid that detail may present us with a brand new ball game."

"What do you want me to do exactly?" Sharon asks.

"Help me," Hayward says.

"Well," says Sharon, after a moment, opening her purse, then opening her wallet, carefully placing the bits of paper in her wallet, closing the wallet, burying the wallet in the depths of her purse, and snapping shut the purse, "then I'll be leaving sometime tomorrow. I'll call, or have somebody call, before I go. Just so you'll know where I am."

And she rises, and Hayward rises, and we walk to the door.

"Do you have a photograph of Fonny with you?" Hayward asks.

"I do," I say.

And I open my bag and find my wallet. I actually have two photographs, one of Fonny and me leaning against the railing of the house on Bank Street. His shirt is open to the belly button, he has one arm around me, and we are both laughing. The other is of Fonny alone, sitting in the house near the record player, somber and peaceful; and it's my favorite photograph of him.

Mama takes the photographs, hands them to Hayward, who studies them. Then she takes them back from Hayward.

"These the only ones you got?" she asks me.

"Yes," I say.

She hands me back the photograph of Fonny alone. She puts the one of Fonny and me into her wallet, which again descends into the bottom of her purse. "This one ought to get it," she says. "After all, it *is* my daughter, and *she* ain't been raped." She shakes hands with Hayward. "Keep your fingers crossed, son, and let's hope the old lady can bring home the goods."

She turns toward the door. But Hayward checks her again.

"The fact that you are going to Puerto Rico makes me feel better than I have felt for weeks. But: I must also tell you that the D.A.'s office is in constant touch with the Hunt family—that is, the mother and the two sisters—and their position appears to be that Fonny has always been incorrigible and worthless."

Hayward pauses, and looks steadily at us both.

"Now: if the state can get three respectable black women to depose, or to testify, that their son and brother has always been a dangerously antisocial creature, this is a very serious blow for us."

He pauses again, and he turns toward the window.

"As a matter of fact—for Galileo Santini is not a stupid man—it might be vastly more effective if he does not call them as character witnesses, for then they cannot be cross-examined—he need merely convey to the jury that these respectable churchgoing women are prostrate with shame and grief. And the father can be dismissed as a hard-drinking good-for-nothing, a dreadful example to his son—especially as he has publicly threatened to blow Santini's head off."

He turns from the window, to watch us very carefully.

"I think I will probably call on you, Sharon, and on Mr. Rivers, as character witnesses. But you see what we are up against."

"It's always better," says Sharon, "to know than not to know."

Hayward claps Sharon gently on the shoulder. "So try to bring home the goods."

I think to myself: and I will take care of those sisters, and that mother. But I don't say anything, except "Thanks, Hayward. Good-bye."

And Sharon says, "Okay. Got you. Good-bye." And we walk down the hall to the elevator.

I remember the night the baby was conceived because it was the night of the day we finally found our loft. And this cat, whose name was Levy, really was going to rent it to us, he wasn't full of shit. He was an olive-skinned, curly-haired, merry-faced boy from the Bronx, about thirty-three, maybe, with big, kind of electrical black eyes, and he dug us. He dug people who loved each other. The loft was off Canal Street, and it was big and in pretty good condition. It had two big windows on the street, and the two back windows opened onto a roof, with a railing. There was a room for Fonny to work, and, with all the windows open, you wouldn't die of heat prostration in the summertime. We were very excited about the roof because you could have dinner on it, or serve drinks, or just sit there in the evenings, if you wanted to, with your arms around each other. "Hell," Levy said, "drag out the blankets and sleep on it." He smiled at Fonny. "Make babies on it. That's how *I* got here." What I most remember about him is that he didn't make either of us feel self-conscious. We all laughed together. "You two should have some beautiful babies," he said, "and, take it from me, kids, the world damn sure needs them."

He asked us for only one month in advance, and, about a week later, I took the money over to him. And then, when Fonny got into trouble, he did something very strange, and, I think, very beautiful. He called me and he said that I could have the money back, anytime I wanted it. But, he said, he wouldn't rent that loft to anybody but us. "I can't," he said. "The bastards. That loft stays empty until your man gets out of jail, and I ain't just whistling Dixie, honey." And he gave me his number and asked me please to let him know if there was anything at all he could do. "I want you kids to have your babies. I'm funny that way."

Levy explained and exhibited the somewhat compli- cated structure of locks and keys. Our loft was the top, up three or four stories. The stairs were steep. There was a set of keys for our loft, which had double locks. Then, there was the door at the top of the steps, which locked us away from the rest of the building.

"Man," Fonny asked, "what do we do in case of fire?"

"Oh," said Levy, "I forgot," and he unlocked the doors again and we went back into the loft. He took us onto the roof and led us to the edge, where the railing was. On the far right of the roof the railing opened, extending itself into a narrow catwalk. This railing led to the metal steps, by which steps one descended into the courtyard. Once in this courtyard, which seemed to be closed in by walls, one might wonder what on earth to do: it was something of a trap. Still, one would not have had to leap from the burning building. Once on the ground, one had to hope, merely, not to be buried beneath the flaming, crashing walls.

"Well," said Fonny, carefully holding me by one elbow, and leading me back onto the roof, "I can dig that." We again went through the ritual of the locking of the doors, and descended into the street. "Don't worry about the neighbors," Levy said, "because, after five or six o'clock, you won't have any. All you got between you and the street are small, failing sweatshops."

And we got into the street and he showed us how to lock and unlock the street door.

"Got it?" he asked Fonny.

"Got it," Fonny said.

"Come on. I'll buy you a milk shake."

And we had three milk shakes on the corner, and Levy shook hands, and left us, saying that he had to get home to his wife and kids—two boys, one aged two, one aged three and a half. But before he left us, he said, "Look. I told you not to worry about the neighbors. But watch out for the cops. They're murder."

One of the most terrible, most mysterious things about a life is that a warning can be heeded only in retrospect: too late.

Levy left us, and Fonny and I walked, hand in hand, up the broad, bright, crowded streets, toward the Village, toward our pad. We talked and talked and laughed and laughed. We crossed Houston and started up Sixth Avenue—Avenue of the Americas!—with all those fucking flags on it, which we didn't see. I wanted to stop at one of the markets on Bleecker Street, to buy some tomatoes. We crossed the Avenue of the Americas and started west, on Bleecker. Fonny had one hand around my waist. We stopped at a vegetable stand. I started looking.

Fonny hates shopping. He said, "Wait one minute. I'm going to buy some cigarettes," and he went up the street, just around the corner.

I started picking out the tomatoes, and I remember that I was kind of humming to myself. I started looking around for a scale and for the man or the woman who would weigh the tomatoes for me and tell me what I owed.

Fonny is right about me when he says I'm not very bright. When I first felt this hand on my behind, I thought it was Fonny: then I realized that Fonny would never, never touch me that way, in public.

I turned, my six tomatoes in both hands, and found myself facing a small, young, greasy Italian punk.

"I can sure dig a tomato who digs tomatoes," he said, and he licked his lips, and smiled.

Two things happened in me, all at the same time—three. This was a very crowded street. I knew that Fonny would be back at any moment. I wanted to smash my tomatoes in the boy's face. But no one had really noticed us yet, and I didn't want Fonny to get into a fight. I saw a white cop coming slowly up the street.

I realized that I was black and that the crowded streets were white and so I turned away and walked into the shop, still with my tomatoes in my hands. I found a scale and I put the tomatoes on the scale and I looked around for someone to weigh them, so that I could pay and get out of this store before Fonny came back from around the corner. The cop was now on the other side of the street; and the boy had followed me into the store.

"Hey, sweet tomato. *You* know I dig tomatoes."

And now people *were* watching us. I did not know what to do—the only thing to do was to get out of there before Fonny turned the corner. I tried to move: but the boy blocked my way. I looked around, for someone to help me—people were staring, but no one moved. I decided, in despair, to call the cop. But, when I moved, the boy grabbed my arm. He was, really, probably, just a broken-down junkie—but when he grabbed my arm, I slapped his face and I spat in it: and exactly at that moment, Fonny entered the store.

Fonny grabbed the boy by the hair, knocked him to the ground, picked him up and kicked him in the balls and dragged him to the sidewalk and knocked him down again. I screamed and held on to Fonny with all my might, for I saw that the cop, who had been on the far corner, was now crossing the street, on the run; and the white boy lay bleeding and retching in the gutter. I was sure that the cop intended to kill Fonny; but he could not kill Fonny if I could keep my body between Fonny and this cop; and with all my strength, with all my love, my prayers, and armed with the knowledge that Fonny was not, after all, going to knock *me* to the ground, I held the back of my head against Fonny's chest, held both his wrists between my two hands, and looked up into the face of this cop. I said, "That man—there—attacked me. Right in this store. Right now. Everybody saw it."

No one said a word.

The cop looked at them all. Then, he looked back at me. Then, he looked at Fonny. I could not see Fonny's face. But I could see the cop's face: and I knew that I must not move, nor, if I could possibly help it, allow Fonny to move.

"And where were you," the cop elaborately asked Fonny, "while all this"—his eyes flicked over me in exactly the same way the boy's eyes had—"while all this was going on between junior, there, and"—his eyes took me in again—"and your girl?"

"He was around the corner," I said, "buying cigarettes." For I did not want Fonny to speak.

I hoped that he would forgive me, later.

"Is that so, boy?"

I said, "He's not a boy. Officer."

Now, he looked at me, really looked at me for the first time, and, therefore, for the first time, he really looked at Fonny.

Meanwhile, some people had got junior to his feet.

"You live around here?" the cop asked Fonny.

The back of my head was still on Fonny's chest, but he had released his wrists from my hands.

"Yes," Fonny said, "on Bank Street," and he gave the officer the address.

I knew that, in a moment, Fonny would push me away.

"We're going to take you down, boy," the cop said, "for assault and battery."

I do not know what would now have happened if the Italian lady who ran the store had not spoken up. "Oh, no," she said, "I know both these young people. They shop here very often. What the young lady has told you is the truth. I saw them both, just now, when they came, and I watched her choose her tomatoes and her young man left her and he said he would be right back. I was busy, I could not get to her right away; her tomatoes are still on the scale. And that little good-for-nothing shit over there, he *did* attack her. And he has got exactly what he deserved. What would *you* do if a man attacked *your* wife? if you have one." The crowd snickered, and the cop flushed. "I saw exactly what happened. I am a witness. And I will swear to it."

She and the cop stared at each other.

"Funny way to run a business," he said, and licked his lower lip.

"*You* will not tell *me* how to run my business," she said. "I was on this street before you got here and I will be here when you are gone. Take," she said, gesturing toward the boy now sitting on the curbstone, with some of his friends around him, "that miserable urchin away with you, to Bellevue, or to Rikers' Island—or drop him in the river, he is of no earthly use to anyone. But do not try to frighten *me—basta!*"

I notice, for the first time, that Bell's eyes are blue and that what I can see of his hair is red.

He looks again at me and then again at Fonny.

He licks his lips again.

The Italian lady reenters the store and takes my tomatoes off the scale and puts them in a bag.

"Well," says Bell, staring at Fonny, "be seeing you around."

"You may," says Fonny, "and then again, you may not."

"Not," says the Italian lady, coming back into the street, "if they, or I, see you first." She turns me around and puts the bag of tomatoes into my hands. She is standing between myself and Bell. She stares into my eyes. "You have a good man," she says. "Take him home. Away from these diseased pigs." I look at her. She touches my face. "I have been in America a long time," she says. "I hope I do not die here."

She goes back into her store. Fonny takes the tomatoes from me, and holds the bag in the crook of one arm; the other arm he entwines through mine, interlocking his fingers through mine. We walk slowly away, toward our pad.

"Tish," says Fonny—very quietly; with a dreadful quietness.

I almost know what he is going to say.

"Yes?"

"Don't ever try to protect me again. Don't do that."

I know I am saying the wrong thing: "But you were trying to protect *me*."

"It's not," he says, with the same terrifying quietness, "the same thing, Tish."

And he suddenly takes the bag of tomatoes and smashes them against the nearest wall. Thank God the wall is blank, thank God it is now beginning to be dark. Thank God tomatoes spatter but do not ring.

I know what he is saying. I know he is right. I know I must not say anything. Thank God, he does not let go my hand. I look down at the sidewalk, which I cannot see. I hope he cannot hear my tears.

But he does.

He stops and turns me to him, and he kisses me. He pulls away and looks at me and kisses me again.

"Don't think I don't know you love me. You believe we going to make it?"

Then, I am calm. There are tears on his face, his or

mine, I don't know. I kiss him where our tears fall. I start to say something. He puts one finger on my lips. He smiles his little smile.

"Hush. Don't say a word. I'm going to take you out to dinner. At our Spanish place, you remember? Only, this time, it's got to be on credit."

And he smiles and I smile and we keep on walking.

"We have no money," Fonny says to Pedrocito, when we enter the restaurant, "but we are very hungry. And I will have some money in a couple of days."

"In a couple of days," says Pedrocito, furiously, "that is what they all say! And, furthermore"—striking an incredulous hand to his forehead—"I suppose that you would like to eat *sitting down!*"

"Why, yes," says Fonny, grinning, "if you could arrange it, that would be nice."

"At a *table*, no doubt?" And he stares at Fonny as though he simply cannot believe his eyes.

"Well—I would—yeah—like a table—"

"Ah!" But, "Good evening, Señorita," Pedrocito now says, and smiles at me. "It is for her I do it, you know," he informs Fonny. "It is clear that you do not feed her properly." He leads us to a table and sits us down. "And now, no doubt," he scowls, "you would like two margheritas?"

"Caught me again," says Fonny, and he and Pedrocito laugh and Pedrocito disappears.

Fonny takes my hand in his.

"Hello," he says.

I say, "Hello."

"I don't want you to feel bad about what I said to you before. You a fine, tough chick and I know, hadn't been for you, my brains might be being spattered all over that precinct basement by now."

He pauses, and he lights a cigarette. I watch him.

"So, I don't mean that you did nothing wrong. I guess you did the only thing you could have done. But you got to understand where I'm coming from."

He takes my hands between his again.

"We live in a nation of pigs and murderers. I'm scared every time you out of my sight. And maybe what happened just now was my fault, because I should never have left you alone at that vegetable stand—but I was just so happy, you know, about the loft—I wasn't thinking—"

"Fonny, I've been to that vegetable stand a hundred times, and nothing like that ever happened before. I've got to take care of you—of us. You can't go everywhere I go. How is it *your* fault? That was just some broken-down junkie—"

"Some broken-down white American," Fonny says.

"Well. It's still not *your* fault."

He smiles at me.

"They got us in a trick bag, baby. It's hard, but I just want for you to bear in mind that they can make us lose each other by putting me in the shit—or, they can try to make us lose each other by making *you* try to protect me from it. You see what I mean?"

"Yes," I say, finally, "I see what you mean. And I know that that's true."

Pedrocito returns, with our margheritas.

"We have a specialty tonight," he announces, "very, *very* Spanish, and we are trying it out on all those customers who think Franco is a great man." He looks at Fonny quizzically. "I suppose that you do not exactly qualify—so, for you, I will remove the arsenic. Without the arsenic, it is a little less strong, but it is actually very good, I think you will like it. Do you trust me not to poison you? Anyway, it would be very foolish of me to poison you before you pay your *tremendous* bill. We would immediately go bankrupt." He turns to me. "Will you trust me, Señorita? I assure you that we will prepare it with love."

"Now, watch it, Pete," says Fonny.

"Oh, your mind is like a sewer, you do not deserve so beautiful a girl." And he disappears again.

"That cop," Fonny says, "that cop."

"What about that cop?" But I am suddenly, and I don't know why, as still and as dry as a stone: with fear.

"He's going to try to get me," Fonny says.

"How? You didn't do anything wrong. The Italian lady said so, and she said that she would swear to it."

"That's why he's going to try to get me," Fonny says. "White men don't like it at *all* when a white lady tells them, You a boatful of motherfuckers, and the black cat was right, and you can kiss my ass." He grins. "Because that's what she told him. In front of a whole lot of people. And he couldn't do shit. And he ain't about to forget it."

"Well," I say, "we'll soon be moving downtown, to our loft."

"That's right," he says, and smiles again. Pedrocito arrives, with our specialties.

When two people love each other, when they really love each other, everything that happens between them has something of a sacramental air. They can sometimes seem to be driven very far from each other: I know of no greater torment, no more resounding void—*When your lover has gone!* But tonight, with our vows so mysteriously menaced, and with both of us, though from different angles, placed before this fact, we were more profoundly together than we had ever been before. *Take care of each other*, Joseph had said. *You going to find out it's more than a notion.*

After dinner, and coffee, Pedrocito offered us brandy, and then he left us, in the nearly empty restaurant. Fonny and I just sat there and sipped our brandy, talking a little, holding hands—digging each other. We finished our brandy. Fonny said, "Shall we go?"

"Yes," I said. For I wanted to be alone with him, in his arms.

He signed the check; the last check he was ever to sign there. I have never been allowed to pay it—it has been, they say, misplaced.

We said good-night, and we walked home, with our arms around each other.

There was a patrol car parked across the street from our house, and, as Fonny opened our gate and unlocked our door, it drove off. Fonny smiled, but said nothing. I said nothing.

The baby was <u>conceived</u> that night. I know it. I know it from the way Fonny touched me, held me, entered me. I had never been so open before. And when he started to pull out, I would not let him, I held on to him as tightly as I could, crying and moaning and shaking with him, and felt life, life, his life, inundating me, entrusting itself to me.

Then, we were still. We did not move, because we could not. We held each other so close that we might indeed have been one body. Fonny caressed me and called my name and he fell asleep. I was very proud. I had crossed my river. Now, we were one.

Sharon gets to Puerto Rico on an evening plane. She knows exactly how much money she has, which means that she knows how rapidly she must move against time —which is inexorably moving against her.

She steps down from the plane, with hundreds of others, and crosses the field, under the blue-black sky; and something in the way the stars hang low, something in the way the air caresses her skin, reminds her of that Birmingham she has not seen in so long.

She has brought with her only a small overnight bag, so she need not wait in line for her luggage. Hayward has made a reservation for her in a small hotel in San Juan; and he has written the address on a piece of paper.

He has warned her that it may not be so easy to find a taxi.

But he has not, of course, been able to prepare her for the stunning confusion which reigns at the San Juan airport. So, Sharon stands still for a moment, trying to sort things out.

She is wearing a green summer dress, my mother, and a wide-brimmed, green cloth hat; her handbag over her shoulder, her overnight bag in her hand; she studies the scene.

Her first impression is that everyone appears to be related to each other. This is not because of the way they look, nor is it a matter of language: it is because of the way they relate to each other. There are many colors here, but this does not, at least at the airport, appear to count for very much. Whoever is speaking is shouting— that is the only way to be heard; and everyone is determined to be heard. It is quite impossible to guess who is leaving, who arriving. Entire families appear to have been squatting there for weeks, with all their earthly possessions piled around them—not, Sharon notes, that these possessions towered very high. For the children, the airport appears to be merely a more challenging way of playing house.

Sharon's problems are real and deep. Since she cannot allow these to become desperate, she must now rely on what she can establish of illusion: and the key to illusion is complicity. The world sees what it wishes to see, or, when the chips are down, what you tell it to see: it does not wish to see who, or what, or why you are. Only Sharon knows that she is my mother, only she knows what she is doing in San Juan, with no one to meet her. Before speculation rises too high, she must make it clear that she is a visitor, from up the road— from North America: who, through no fault of her own, speaks no Spanish.

Sharon walks to the Hertz desk, and stands there, and smiles, somewhat insistently, at one of the young ladies behind the desk.

"Do you speak English?" she asks the young lady.

The young lady, anxious to prove that she does, looks up, determined to be helpful.

Sharon hands her the address of the hotel. The young lady looks at it, looks back at Sharon. Her look makes Sharon realize that Hayward has been very thoughtful, and that he has placed her in a very respected, respectable hotel.

"I am very sorry to bother you," says Sharon, "but I do not speak any Spanish, and I have had to come here unexpectedly." She pauses, giving no explanation. "And I do not drive. I wondered if I could rent a car, with a driver, or, if not, if you could tell me exactly how to get a taxi—?" Sharon makes a helpless gesture. "You see—?"

She smiles, and the young lady smiles. She looks again at the paper, looks around the airport, narrowing her eyes.

"One moment, Señora," she says.

She leaves her phone off the hook, swings open the small gate, closes it behind her, and disappears.

She reappears very quickly, with a boy of about eighteen. "This is your taxi driver," she says. "He will take you where you are going." She reads the address aloud, and gives the piece of paper back to Sharon. She smiles. "I hope you will enjoy your visit, Señora. If you need anything—allow me?" She gives Sharon her card. "If you need anything, please do not hesitate to call on me."

"Thank you," says Sharon. "Thank you very much. You have been beautiful."

"It was nothing. Jaime," she says, authoritatively, "take the lady's bag."

Jaime does so, and Sharon says good-night, and follows Jaime.

Sharon thinks, *One down!* and begins to be frightened.

But she has to make her choices very quickly. On the way into town, she decides—because he is there—to make friends with Jaime, and to depend, or to seem to depend, on him. He knows the town, and he can drive. It is true that he is terribly young. But that could turn out to be a plus. Someone older, knowing more, might turn out to be a terrible hassle. Her idea is to case the nightclub, to see Pietro, and, possibly, Victoria, without saying anything to them. But it is not a simple matter for a lone woman, black or white, to walk, unescorted, into a nightclub. Furthermore, for all she knows, this nightclub may be a whorehouse. Her only option is to play the American tourist, wide-eyed—but she is black, and this is Puerto Rico.

Only she knows that she's my mother, and about to become a grandmother; only she knows that she is past forty; only she knows what she is doing here.

She tips Jaime when they arrive at the hotel. Then, as

her bag is carried into the hotel, she looks suddenly at her watch. "My God," she says, "do you think you could wait for me, just for a minute, while I register? I had no *idea* it was so late. I promised to meet someone. I won't be a moment. The boy will carry the bag up. Will that be all right?"

Jaime is a somewhat muddy-faced boy, with brilliant eyes, and a sullen smile. He is entirely intrigued by this improbable North American lady—intrigued because he knows, through unutterably grim experience, that, though she may be in trouble, and certainly has a secret, she is not attempting to do him any violence. He understands that she needs him—the taxi—for something; but that is not his affair. He does not know he knows it—the thought has not consciously entered his mind—but he knows she is a mother. He has a mother. He knows one when he sees one. He knows, again without knowing that he knows it, that he can be of service to her tonight. His courtesy is as real as her trouble. And so he says, gravely, that, of course, he will take the Señora where-ever she wishes and wait for her as long as she likes.

Sharon cheats on him, a little. She registers, goes up in the elevator with the bellboy, tips him. She cannot decide whether to wear her hat, or not. Her problem is both trivial and serious, but she has never had to confront it before. Her problem is that she does not look her age. She takes her hat off. She puts it back on. Does the hat make her look younger, or older? At home, she looks her age (whatever that age is) because everybody knows her age. She looks her age because she knows her role. But, now, she is about to enter a nightclub, in a strange town, for the first time in twenty years, alone. She puts the hat on. She takes it off. She realizes that panic is about to overtake her, and so she throws the hat onto the night table, scrubs her face in cold water as harshly as she once scrubbed mine, puts on a high-necked white blouse and a black skirt and black high-heeled shoes, pulls her hair cruelly back from her forehead, knots it, and throws a black shawl over her head and shoulders. The intention of all this is to make her look elderly. The effect is to make her look juvenile. Sharon curses, but the taxi is waiting. She grabs her handbag, runs to the elevator, walks swiftly through the lobby, and gets to the taxi. She, certainly, anyway, Jaime's brilliant eyes inform her, looks like a Yankee—or a *gringo*—tourist.

The nightclub is located in what was certainly a back-water, if not, indeed, a swamp, before the immense hotel which houses it was built. It is absolutely hideous, so loud, so blatant, so impervious and cruel, that, facing it causes mere vulgarity to seem an irrecoverable state of grace. Sharon is now really frightened, her hands are shaking. She lights a cigarette.

"I must find someone," she says, to Jaime. "I will not be long."

She has no way of realizing, at that moment, that the entire militia would have trouble driving Jaime away. Sharon has now become his property. This lady, he knows, is in deep trouble. And it is not an ordinary trouble: because this *is* a lady.

"Certainly, Señora," says Jaime, with a smile, and gets out of the cab, and comes to open the door for her.

"Thank you," Sharon says, and walks quickly toward the garish doors, wide open. There is no doorman visible. But there will certainly be a doorman inside.

Now, it must all be played by ear. And all that holds her up, my mother, who once dreamed of being a singer, is her private knowledge of what she is doing in this place.

She enters, in fact, the hotel lobby, keys, registration, mail, cashier, bored clerks (mainly white, and decidedly pale) with no one paying her the slightest attention. She walks as though she knows exactly where she is going. The nightclub is on the left, down a flight of stairs. She turns left, and walks down the stairs.

No one has stopped her yet.

"Señorita—?"

She has never seen a photograph of Pietro. The man before her is bland and swarthy. The light is too dim (and her surroundings too strange) for her to be able to guess his age; he does not seem unfriendly. Sharon smiles.

"Good evening. I hope I'm in the right place. This is —?" and she stammers the name of the nightclub.

"Sí, Señorita."

"Well—I'm supposed to meet a friend here, but the flight I meant to take was overbooked, and so I was forced to take an earlier one. So, I'm a little early. Could you hide me at a table, in a corner, somewhere?"

"Certainly. With pleasure." He leads her through the crowded room. "What is the name of your friend?"

Her mind dries up, she must go for broke. "It's actually more in the nature of business. I am waiting for a Señor Alvarez. I am Mrs. Rivers. From New York."

"Thank you." He seats her at a table, against the wall. "Will you have a drink while waiting?"

"Yes. Thank you. A screwdriver."

He bows, whoever he is, and walks away.

Two down! thinks Sharon. And she is now very calm.

This is a nightclub, and so the music is—"live." Sharon's days with the drummer come back to her. Her days as a singer come back to her. They do not, as she is to make very vivid to me, much later, come back with the rind of regret. She and the drummer lost each other —that was that; she was not equipped to be a singer, and that was that. Yet, she remembers what she and the drummer and the band attempted, she knows from whence they came. If I remember "Uncloudy Day" because I remember myself sitting on my mother's knee when I first heard it, she remembers "My Lord and I": *And so, we'll walk together, my Lord and I.* That song is Birmingham, her father and her mother, the kitchens, and the mines. She may never, in fact, ever have particularly liked that particular song, but she knows about it, it is a part of her. She slowly realizes that this is the song, which, to different words, if words indeed there are, the young people on the bandstand are belting, or bolting out. And they know nothing at all about the song they are singing: which causes Sharon to wonder if they know anything about themselves at all. This is the first time that Sharon has been alone in a very long time. Even now, she is alone merely physically, in the same way, for example, that she is alone when she goes shopping for her family. Shopping, she must listen, she must look, say yes to this, say no to that, she must choose: she has a family to feed. She cannot poison them, because she loves them. And now she finds herself listening to a sound she has never heard before. If she were shopping, she could not take this home and put it on the family table for it would not nourish them. *My gal and I!* cries the undernourished rock singer, whipping himself into an electronic orgasm. But no one who had ever had a lover, a mother or father, or a Lord, could sound so despairingly masturbatory. For it is despair that Sharon is hearing, and despair, whether or not it can be taken home and placed on the family table, must always be respected. Despair can make one monstrous, but it can also make one noble: and here these children are, in the arena, up for grabs. Sharon claps for them, because she prays for them. Her screwdriver comes, and she smiles up at a face she cannot see. She sips her drink. She stiffens: the children are about to go into their next number: and she looks up into another face she cannot see.

The children begin their number, loud: "I Can't Get No Satisfaction."

"You Mrs. Rivers? You waiting for me?"

"I think so. Won't you sit down?"

He sits down, facing her. Now, she sees him.

Again—thinking of me, and Fonny, and the baby, cursing herself for being so inept, knowing herself to be encircled, trapped, her back to the wall, his back to the door—she yet must go for broke.

"I was told that a certain Mr. Pietro Alvarez worked here. Are you Pietro Alvarez?"

She sees him. And yet, of course, at the same time, she doesn't.

"Maybe. What you want to see him about?"

Sharon wants a cigarette, but she is afraid her hand will tremble. She picks up her screwdriver in both hands, and sips it, slowly, rather thanking God, now, for the shawl, which she can maneuver to shadow her face. If she can see him, he can also see her. She is silent for a moment. Then she puts down her drink and she picks up a cigarette.

"May I have a light, please?"

He lights it. She takes off the shawl.

"I do not especially want to see Mr. Alvarez. I want to see Mrs. Victoria Rogers. I am the mother-in-law, to be, of the man she has accused of raping her, and who is now in prison, in New York."

She watches him. He watches her. Now, she begins to see him.

"Well, lady, you got one hell of a son-in-law, let me tell you that."

"I also have one hell of a daughter. Let *me* tell you *that*."

The moustache he has grown to make him look older twitches. He runs his hands through his thick black hair.

"Look. The kid's been through enough. More than enough. Leave her alone."

"A man is about to die, for something he didn't do. Can we leave *him* alone?"

"What makes you think he didn't do it?"

"*Look at me!*"

The children on the bandstand finish their set, and go off, and, immediately, the jukebox takes over: Ray Charles, "I Can't Stop Loving You."

"What you want me to look at you for?"

The waiter comes.

"What are you drinking? Señor?" Sharon put out her cigarette, and immediately lights another.

"It's on me. Give me the usual. And give the lady what she's drinking."

The waiter goes.

"Look at me."

"I'm looking at you."

"Do you think I love my daughter?"

"Frankly—it's hard to believe you *have* a daughter."

"I'm about to become a grandmother."

"From—?"

"Yes."

He is young, very, very young, but also very old; but not old in the way that she had expected him to be. She had expected the age of corruption. She is confronting the age of sorrow. She is confronting torment.

"Do you think that I would marry my daughter to a rapist?"

"You might not know."

"Look at me again."

And he does. But it does not help him.

"Look. I wasn't there. But Victoria swears it was him. And she's been through shit, baby, she's been through some *shit,* and I don't want to put her through no more! I'm sorry, lady, but I don't care what happens to your daughter—" He stops. "She's going to have a baby?"

"Yes."

"What you want from me? Can't you leave us alone? We just want to be left alone."

Sharon says nothing.

"Look. I ain't no American. You got all them lawyers and folks up there, why you coming to me? Shit—I'm sorry, but I ain't nothing. I'm an Indian, wop, spic, spade —name it, that's me. I got my little thing going here, and I got Victoria, and, lady, I don't want to put her through no more shit; I'm sorry, lady, but I really just can't help you."

He starts to rise—he does not want to cry before her. Sharon takes his wrist. He sits down, one hand before his face.

Sharon takes out her wallet.

"Pietro—I can call you that, because I am old enough to be your mother. My son-in-law is your age."

He leans his head on one hand, and looks at her.

Sharon hands him the photograph of Fonny and myself.

"Look at it."

He does not want to, but he does.

"Are you a rapist?"

He looks up at her.

"Answer me. Are you?"

The dark eyes, in the stolid face, staring, now directly into my mother's eyes, make the face electrical, light a fire in the darkness of a far-off hill: he has heard the question.

"Are you?"

"No."

"Do you think I have come here to make you suffer?"

"No."

"Do you think I am a liar?"

"No."

"Do you think I am crazy?—we are all a little crazy, I know. But *really* crazy?"

"No."

"Then, will you take this photograph home, to Victoria, and ask her really to think about it, really to study it? Hold her in your arms. Do that. I am a woman. I know that she was raped, and I know—well—I know what women know. But I also *know* that Alonzo did not rape her. And I say that, to you, because I know that you know what men know. *Hold her in your arms.*" She stares at him an instant; he stares at her. "And—will you call me tomorrow?" She gives him the name and the phone number of the hotel. He writes it down. "Will you?"

He looks at her, now very hard and cold. He looks at the phone number. He looks at the photograph.

He pushes both toward Sharon.

"No," he says, and rises, and leaves.

Sharon sits there. She listens to the music. She watches the dancers. She forces herself to finish her second, unwanted drink. She cannot believe that what is happening is actually happening. But it *is* happening. She lights a cigarette. She is acutely aware, not merely of her color, but of the fact that in the sight of so many witnesses, her position, ambiguous upon her entrance, is now absolutely clear: the twenty-two-year-old boy she has traveled so far to see has just walked out on her. She wants to cry. She also wants to laugh. She signals for the waiter.

"Sí—?"

"What do I owe you?"

The waiter looks bewildered. "But nothing, Señora. Señor Alvarez has made himself responsible."

She realizes that his eyes hold neither pity, nor scorn. This is a great shock to her, and it brings tears to her eyes. To hide this, she bows her head and arranges her shawl. The waiter moves away. Sharon leaves five dollars on the table. She walks to the door. The bland, swarthy man opens it for her.

"Thank you, Señora. Good-night. Your taxi is waiting for you. Please come again."

"Thank you," my mother says, and smiles, and walks up the stairs.

She walks through the lobby. Jaime is leaning against the taxi. His face brightens when he sees her, and he opens the door for her.

"What time will you need me tomorrow?" he asks her.

"Is nine o'clock too early?"

"But, no." He laughs. "I am always up before six."

The car begins to move.

"Beautiful," says Sharon—swinging her foot, thinking ahead.

And the baby starts kicking, waking me up at night. Now that Mama is in Puerto Rico, it is Ernestine and Joseph who keep watch over me. I am afraid to quit my job, because I know we need the money. This means that I very often miss the six o'clock visit.

It seems to me that if I quit my job, I'll be making the six o'clock visit forever. I explain this to Fonny, and he says he understands, and, in fact, he does. But understanding doesn't help him at six o'clock. No matter what you understand, you can't help waiting: for your name to be called, to be taken from your cell and led downstairs. If you have visitors, or even if you have only one visitor, but that visitor is constant, it means that someone outside cares about you. And this can get you through the night, into the day. No matter what you may understand, and *really* understand, and no matter what you may tell yourself, if no one comes to see you, you are in very bad trouble. And trouble, here, means danger.

Joseph puts it to me very squarely, one Sunday morning. I have been more than usually sick that morning, and Joseph has had to tend to me because Ernestine has a rush job at the home of the actress. I cannot imagine what this thing inside of me is doing, but it appears to have acquired feet. Sometimes it is still, for days on end,

sleeping perhaps, but more probably plotting—plotting
its escape. Then, it turns, beating the water, churning,
obviously becoming unspeakably bored in this element,
and wanting out. We are beginning to have a somewhat
acrid dialogue, this thing and I—it kicks, and I smash an
egg on the floor, it kicks, and suddenly the coffeepot is
upside down on the table, it kicks, and the perfume on
the back of my hand brings salt to the roof of my mouth,
and my free hand weighs on the heavy glass counter,
with enough force to crack it in two. Goddammit. Be
patient. I'm doing the best I can—and it kicks again,
delighted to have elicited so furious a response. Please.
Be still. And then, exhausted, or, as I suspect, merely
cunning, it *is* still, having covered my forehead with
sweat, and having caused me to vomit up my breakfast,
and go to the bathroom—uselessly—about four or five
times. But it really *is* very cunning, it intends to live: it
never moves while I am riding the subway, or when I am
crossing a crowded street. But it grows heavier and heavier, its claims become more absolute with every hour. It
is, in fact, staking its claim. The message is that it does
not so much belong to *me*—though there is another,
gentler kick, usually at night, signifying that it has no
objection to belonging to me, that we may even grow to
be fond of each other—as *I* belong to *it*. And then it hauls
off again, like Muhammad Ali, and I am on the ropes.

I do not recognize my body at all, it is becoming absolutely misshapen. I try not to look at it, because I simply do not recognize it. Furthermore, I sometimes take
something off in the evening, and have difficulty getting

back into it in the morning. I can no longer wear high heels, they distort my sense of balance as profoundly as one's vision is distorted if one is blind in one eye. I have never had breasts, or a behind, but I am beginning to have them now. It seems to me that I am gaining weight at the rate of about three hundred pounds an hour, and I do not dare speculate on what I will probably look like by the time this thing inside of me finally kicks itself out. Lord. And yet, we are beginning to know each other, this thing, this creature, and I, and sometimes we are very, very friendly. It has something to say to me, and I must learn to listen—otherwise, I will not know what to say when it gets here. And Fonny would never forgive me for that. After all, it was I who wanted this baby, more than he. And, at a depth beneath and beyond all our troubles, I am very happy. I can scarcely smoke at all anymore, *it* has seen to that. I have acquired a passion for cocoa, and doughnuts, and brandy is the only alcohol which has any taste at all. So, Ernestine casually brings over a few bottles from the actress's house. "She'll never miss them, baby. The way *they* drink?"

On this Sunday morning, Joseph serves me my third cup of cocoa, the previous two having been kicked right back up, and sits down at the table before me, very stern.

"Do you want to bring this baby here, or not?"

The way he looks at me, and the way he sounds, scares me half to death.

"Yes," I say, "I do."

"And you love Fonny?"

"Yes. I do."

"Then, I'm sorry, but you going to have to quit your job."

I watch him.

"I know you worried about the money. But you let *me* worry about that. I got more experience. Anyway, you ain't making no damn money. All you doing is wearing yourself out, and driving Fonny crazy. You keep on like you going, you going to lose that baby. You lose that baby, and Fonny won't want to live no more, and you'll be lost and then I'll be lost, everything is lost."

He stands up and walks to the window, his back to me. Then, he faces me again. "I'm serious, Tish."

I say, "I know you are."

Joseph smiles. "Listen, little girl. We got to take care of each other in this world, right? Now: there are some things I can do that you can't do. That's all. There's things *I* can do that *you can't do*—and things *you* can do that *I* can't do, just like I can't have your baby for you. I would if I could. There's nothing I wouldn't do for you— you know that?" And he watches me, still smiling.

"Yes. I know that."

"And there are things *you* can do for Fonny that I can't do—right?"

"Yes."

Joseph walks up and down the kitchen. "Young folks hate to hear this—I did, when I was young—but you *are* young. Child, I wouldn't lose neither one of you for all the goddamn coffee in Brazil—but you young. Fonny ain't hardly much more than a boy. And he's in trouble no boy should be in. And you all he's got, Tish. You are *all* he's got. I'm a man, and I know what I'm talking about. You understand me?"

"Yes."

He sits down before me again. "You got to see him every day, Tish. Every day. You take care of Fonny. We'll take care of the rest. All right?"

"All right."

He kisses my tears.

"Get that baby here, safe and sound. We'll get Fonny out of jail. I promise. Do *you* promise?"

I smile, and I say, "Yes. I promise."

The next morning, I am, anyway, far too ill to be able to go to work and Ernestine calls the store to tell them so. She says that she, or I, will be coming in to collect my paycheck in the next few days.

So, that is that, and here we go. There is a level on which, if I'm to be honest, I must say that I absolutely hated it—: having nothing to do. But this forced me to recognize, finally, that I had clung to my job in order to avoid my trouble. Now, I was alone, with Fonny, my baby, and me.

But Joseph was right, and Fonny is radiant. On the days I do not see Hayward, I see Fonny twice a day. I am always there for the six o'clock visit. And Fonny knows that I will be there. It is very strange, and I now begin to learn a very strange thing. My presence, which is of no practical value whatever, which can even be considered, from a practical point of view, as a betrayal, is vastly more important than any practical thing I might be doing. Every day, when he sees my face, he knows, again, that I love him—and God knows I do, more and more, deeper and deeper, with every hour. But it isn't only that. It means that others love him, too, love him so much that they have set me free to be there. He is not alone; we are not alone. And if I am somewhat terrified by the fact that I no longer have anything which can be called a waistline, he is delighted. "Here she come! Big as *two* houses! You sure it ain't twins? or triplets? Shit, we *might* make history."

Throwing back his head, holding on to the telephone, looking me in the eye, laughing.

And I understand that the growth of the baby is connected with his determination to be free. So. I don't care if I get to be as big as two houses. The baby wants out. Fonny wants out. And we are going to make it: in time.

Jaime is prompt, and Sharon is in the *favella* by nine thirty. Jaime knows the location, roughly, of the particular dwelling, but he does not know the lady—at least, he is not sure that he does. He is still thinking about it when Sharon steps out of the taxi.

Hayward had tried to warn Sharon by telling her that he had never been able to describe a *favella* and that he very much doubted, if, after her visit, she would wish to try. It is bitter. The blue sky above, and the bright sun; the blue sea, here, the garbage dump, there. It takes a moment to realize that the garbage dump *is* the *favella*. Houses are built on it—dwellings; some on stilts, as though attempting to rise above the dung heap. Some have corrugated metal roofs. Some have windows. All have children.

Jaime walks beside Sharon, proud to be her protector, uneasy about the errand. The smell is fantastic—but the children, sliding up and down their mountain, making the air ring, dark, half naked, with their brilliant eyes, their laughter, splashing into and out of the sea, do not seem to care.

"This ought to be the place," Jaime says, and Sharon steps through an archway into a crumbling courtyard. The house which faces her must have been, at some point in time, an extremely important private dwelling. It is not private now. Generations of paint flake off the walls, and the sunlight, which reveals every stain and crack, does not deign to enter the rooms: some of which are shuttered, to the extent, that is, that the shutters hold. It is louder than an untrained orchestra in rehearsal and the sound of infants and children is the theme: tremendously developed, in extraordinary harmonies, in the voices of the elders. There seem to be doors everywhere—low, dark, and square.

"I think it might be here," Jaime says, nervously, and he points to one of the doors. "On the third floor. I think. You say she is blond?"

Sharon looks at him. He is absolutely miserable: he does not want her to go upstairs alone.

She touches his face, and smiles: he suddenly reminds her of Fonny, brings back to her why she is here.

"Wait for me," she says. "Don't worry. I won't be long."

And she walks through the door and climbs the steps as though she knows exactly where she is going. There are four doors on the third floor. There are no names on any of them. One of them is a little open, and she knocks on it—opening it a little further as she knocks.

"Mrs. Rogers—?"

A very thin girl, with immense dark eyes in a dark face, wearing a flowered housedress, barefoot, steps into the middle of the room. Her curly hair is a muddy blond: high cheekbones, thin lips, wide mouth: a gentle, vulnerable, friendly face. A gold crucifix burns against her throat.

She says, "Señora—?" and then stands still, staring at Sharon with her great eyes, frightened.

"Señora—?"

For Sharon has said nothing, merely stands in the doorway, watching her.

The girl's tongue moistens her lips. She says, again, "Señora—?"

She does not look her age. She looks like a little girl. Then she moves and the light strikes her differently and Sharon recognizes her.

Sharon leans against the open door, really afraid for a moment that she will fall.

"Mrs. Rogers—?"

The girl's eyes narrow, her lips curl.

"No, Señora. You are mistaken. I am Sanchez."

They watch each other. Sharon is still leaning against the door.

The girl makes a movement toward the door, as though

to close it. But she does not wish to push Sharon. She does not want to touch her. She takes one step, she stops; she touches the crucifix at her throat, staring at Sharon. Sharon cannot read the girl's face. There is concern in it, not unlike Jaime's concern. There is terror in it, too, and a certain covered terrified sympathy.

Sharon, still not absolutely certain that she can move, yet senses that whether she can move or not, it is better not to change her position against the open door. It gives her some kind of advantage.

"Excuse me, Señora, but I have work to do—if you please? I don't know any Mrs. Rogers. Maybe in one of the other places around here—?" She smiles faintly and looks toward the open window. "But there are so many. You will be looking for a long time."

She looks at Sharon, with bitterness. Sharon straightens and they are, abruptly, looking each other in the eye—each held, now, by the other.

"I have a photograph of you," says Sharon.

The girl says nothing. She attempts to look amused.

Sharon takes out the photograph and holds it up. The girl walks toward the door. As she advances, Sharon moves from the door, into the room.

"Señora—! I have told you that I have my work to do." She looks Sharon up and down. "I am not a North American lady."

"I am not a lady. I am Mrs. Rivers."

"And I am Mrs. Sanchez. What do you want with me? I do not know you."

"I know you don't *know* me. Maybe you never even

heard of me." Something happens in the girl's face, she tightens her lips, rummages in the pocket of her housecoat for her cigarettes, blowing the smoke insolently toward Sharon. Yet, "Will you have a cigarette, Señora?" and she extends the package toward Sharon.

There is a plea in the girl's eyes, and Sharon, with a shaking hand, takes the cigarette and the girl lights it for her. She puts the package back into the pocket of her housecoat.

"I know you don't know me. But I think you must have heard of me."

The girl looks briefly at the photograph in Sharon's hand; looks at Sharon; and says nothing.

"I met Pietro last night."

"Ah! And did he give you the photograph?"

She had meant this as sarcasm; realizes that she made a mistake; still—her defiant eyes seem to say, staring into Sharon's—there are so many Pietros!

"No. I got it from the lawyer for Alonzo Hunt—the man you say raped you."

"I don't know what you're talking about."

"I think you do."

"Look. I ain't got nothing against nobody. But I got to ask you to get out of here."

She is trembling, and close to tears. She holds both dark hands clenched tightly before her, as though to prevent herself from touching Sharon.

"I'm here to try to get a man out of *prison*. That man is going to marry my daughter. And he did not rape you."

She takes out the photograph of me and Fonny.

"Look at it."

The girl turns away, again toward the window; sits down on the unmade bed, still staring out of the window.

Sharon approaches her.

"Look at it. Please. The girl is my daughter. The man with her is Alonzo Hunt. Is this the man who raped you?"

The girl will not look at the photograph, or at Sharon.

"Is this the man who raped you?"

"One thing I can tell, lady—you ain't never been raped." She looks down at the photograph, briefly, then up at Sharon, briefly. "It looks like him. But he wasn't laughing."

After a moment, Sharon asks, "May I sit down?"

The girl says nothing, only sighs and folds her arms. Sharon sits beside her, on the bed.

There must be two thousand transistor radios playing all around them, and all of them are playing B.B. King. Actually, Sharon cannot tell what the radios are playing, but she recognizes the beat: it has never sounded louder, more insistent, more plaintive. It has never before sounded so determined and dangerous. This beat is echoed in the many human voices, and corroborated by the sea—which shines and shines beyond the garbage heap of the *favella*.

Sharon sits and listens, listens like she never has before. The girl's face is turned toward the window. Sharon wonders what she is hearing, what she is seeing. Perhaps she is not seeing or hearing anything. She sits with a stubborn, still helplessness, her thin hands limp between her knees, like one who has been caught in traps before.

Sharon watches her fragile back. The girl's curly hair is beginning to dry out, and is dark at the roots. The beat of the music rises higher, becoming almost unbearable, beginning to sound inside Sharon's head, and causing her to feel that her mind is about to crack.

She is very close to tears now, she cannot tell herself why. She rises from the bed, and walks toward the music. She looks at the children, and watches the sea. In the distance there is an archway, not unlike the archway through which she has walked, abandoned by the Moors. She turns and looks at the girl. The girl is looking down at the floor.

"Were you born here?" Sharon asks her.

"Look, lady, before you go any further, just let me tell you, you can't do nothing to me, I ain't alone and helpless here, I got friends, just let me tell you!"

And she flashes up at Sharon a furious, frightened, doubting look. But she does not move.

"I'm not trying to do anything to you. I'm just trying to get a man out of jail."

The girl turns on the bed, putting her back to Sharon.

"An innocent man," Sharon adds.

"Lady, I think you in the wrong place, I really do. Ain't no reason to talk to me. Ain't nothing I can do!"

Sharon begins searching:

"How long were you in New York?"

The girl flicks her cigarette out of the window. "Too long."

"Did you leave your children there?"

"Listen. Leave my children out of this."

It is getting hot in the room, and Sharon takes off her light cloth jacket and sits down again on the bed.

"I," she says, carefully, "am a mother, too."

The girl looks at her, attempting a scornful distance. But, though she and envy are familiars, scorn is unknown to her.

"Why did you come back here?" Sharon asks her.

This is not the question which the girl had expected. In fact, it is not the question which Sharon had intended to ask.

And they look at each other, the question shimmering between them the way the light changes on the sea.

"You said you're a mother," the girl says, finally, and rises and walks again to the window.

This time, Sharon follows her, and they stare out at the sea together. In a way, with the girl's sullen answer, Sharon's mind begins to clear. In the girl's answer she reads a plea: she begins to speak to her differently.

"Daughter. In this world, terrible things happen to you, and we can all do some terrible things." She is carefully looking out of the window; she is watching the girl. "I was a woman before you got to be a woman. Remember that. But"—and she turns to Victoria, she pulls the girl toward her, the thin wrists, the bony hands, the folded arms, touching her, lightly: she tries to speak as though she were speaking to me—"you pay for the lies you tell." She stares at the girl. The girl stares at her. "You've put a man in jail, daughter, a man you've never seen. He's twenty-two years old, daughter, he wants to marry *my* daughter—and—" Victoria's eyes meet hers again—"he's black." She lets the girl go, and turns back to the window. "Like us."

"I *did* see him."

"You saw him in the police lineup. That's the *first* time you saw him. And the *only* time."

"What makes *you* so sure?"

"Because I've known him all his life."

"Hah!" says Victoria, and tries to move away. Tears rise in the dark, defeated eyes. "If you knew how many women I've heard say that. They didn't see him—when *I* saw him—when he came to *me!* They *never* see that. Respectable *women*—like you!—they never see that." The tears begin to roll down her face. "You might have known a nice little boy, and he might be a nice man—with *you!* But you don't know the man who did—who did—what he did to *me!*"

"But, are you," Sharon asks, "sure that *you* know him?"

"*Yes*, I'm sure. They took me down there and they asked me to pick him out and I picked him out. That's all."

"But you were—it happened—in the dark. You saw Alonzo Hunt—in the lights."

"There's lights in the hallway. I saw enough."

Sharon grabs her again, and touches the crucifix.

"Daughter, daughter. In the name of God."

Victoria looks down at the hand on the cross, and screams: a sound like no sound Sharon has ever heard before. She breaks away from Sharon, and runs to the door, which has remained open all this time. She is screaming and crying, "Get out of here! Get out of here!"

Doors open. People begin to appear. Sharon hears the taxi horn. *One: two: one: two: one: two: three: one: two: three.* Victoria is now screaming in Spanish. One of the older women in the hall comes to the door, and takes Victoria in her arms. Victoria collapses, weeping, into this woman's breasts; and the woman, without a look at Sharon, leads her away. But everyone else, gathering, is staring at Sharon and now the lonely sound Sharon hears is the horn of Jaime's taxi.

They are staring at her, at her clothes; there is nothing she can say to them; she moves into the hallway, toward them. Her light summer jacket is over her arm, she is holding her handbag, she has the photograph of Fonny and me in one hand. She gets past them slowly, and, slowly, gets down the staring stairs. There are people on every landing. She gets out of the courtyard, into the street. Jaime opens the taxi door for her. She gets in, he slams the door, and, without a word, he drives her away.

In the evening, she goes to the club. But, the doorman informs her, Señor Alvarez will not be there this evening, that there are no tables for single women, and that, anyway, the club is full.

The mind is like an object that picks up dust. The object doesn't know, any more than the mind does, why what clings to it clings. But once whatever it is lights on you, it doesn't go away; and so, after that afternoon at the vegetable stand, I saw Bell everywhere, and all the time.

I did not know his name then. I discovered his name on the night I asked him for it. I had already memorized his badge number.

I had certainly seen him before that particular afternoon, but he had been just another cop. After that afternoon, he had red hair and blue eyes. He was somewhere in his thirties. He walked the way John Wayne walks, striding out to clean up the universe, and he believed all that shit: a wicked, stupid, infantile motherfucker. Like his heroes, he was kind of pinheaded, heavy gutted, big assed, and his eyes were as blank as George Washington's eyes. But I was beginning to learn something about the blankness of those eyes. What I was learning was beginning to frighten me to death. If you look steadily into that unblinking blue, into that pinpoint at the center of the eye, you discover a bottomless cruelty, a viciousness cold and icy. In that eye, you do not exist: if you are lucky. If that eye, from its height, has been forced to notice you, if you *do* exist in the unbelievably frozen winter which lives behind that eye, you are marked, marked, marked, like a man in a black overcoat, crawling, fleeing, across the snow. The eye resents your presence in the landscape, cluttering up the view. Presently, the black overcoat will be still, turning red with blood, and the snow will be red, and the eye resents this, too, blinks once, and causes more snow to fall, covering it all. Sometimes I was with Fonny when I crossed Bell's path, sometimes I was alone. When I was with Fonny, the eyes looked straight ahead, into a freezing sun. When I was alone, the eyes clawed me like a cat's claws, raked me like a rake. These eyes look only into the eyes of the conquered victim. They cannot look into any other eyes. When Fonny was alone, the same thing happened. Bell's eyes swept over Fonny's black body with the unanswerable cruelty of lust, as though he had lit the blowtorch and had it aimed at Fonny's sex. When their paths crossed, and I was there, Fonny looked straight at Bell, Bell looked straight ahead. *I'm going to fuck you, boy*, Bell's eyes said. *No, you won't*, said Fonny's eyes. *I'm going to get my shit together and haul ass out of here.*

I was frightened because, in the streets of the Village, I realized that we were entirely alone. Nobody cared about us except us; or, whoever loved us was not there.

Bell spoke to me once. I was making it to Fonny's, late, from work. I was surprised to see him because I had got off the subway at Fourteenth Street and Eighth Avenue, and he was usually in the neighborhood of Bleecker and MacDougal. I was huffing and puffing down the avenue, carrying a package of odds and ends I had lifted from the Jew, when I saw him walking slowly up the avenue, toward me. For a minute, I was frightened because my package—which had things like glue and staples and watercolors and paper and tacks and nails and pens—was hot. But he couldn't know that, and I already hated him too much to care. I walked toward him, he walked toward me. It was beginning to be dark, around seven, seven thirty. The streets were full, homeward men, leaning drunkards, fleeing women, Puerto Rican kids, junkies: here came Bell.

"Can I carry that for you?"

I almost dropped it. In fact, I almost peed on myself. I looked into his eyes.

"No," I said, "thanks very much," and I tried to keep moving, but he was standing in my way.

I looked into his eyes again. This may have been the very first time I ever really looked into a white man's eyes. It stopped me, I stood still. It was not like looking into a man's eyes. It was like nothing I knew, and—therefore—it was very powerful. It was seduction which contained the promise of rape. It was rape which promised debasement and revenge: on both sides. I wanted to get close to him, to enter into him, to open up that face and change it and destroy it, descend into the slime with him. Then, we would both be free: I could almost hear the singing.

"Well," he said, in a very low voice, "you ain't got far to go. Sure wish I could carry it for you, though."

I can still see us on that hurrying, crowded, twilight avenue, me with my package and my handbag, staring at him, he staring at me. I was suddenly his: a desolation entered me which I had never felt before. I watched his eyes, his moist, boyish, despairing lips, and felt his sex stiffening against me.

"I ain't a bad guy," he said. "Tell your friend. You ain't got to be afraid of me."

"I'm not afraid," I said. "I'll tell him. Thanks."

"Good-night," he said.

"Good-night," I answered, and I hurried on my way.

I never told Fonny about it. I couldn't. I blotted it out of my mind. I don't know if Bell ever spoke to Fonny—I doubt it.

On the night that Fonny was arrested, Daniel was at the house. He was a little drunk. He was crying. He was talking, again, about his time in prison. He had seen nine men rape one boy: and *he* had been raped. He would never, never, never again be the Daniel he had been. Fonny held him, held him up just before he fell. I went to make the coffee.

And then they came knocking at the door.

TWO

Zion

Fonny is working on the wood. It is a soft, brown wood, it stands on his worktable. He has decided to do a bust of me. The wall is covered with sketches. I am not there.

His tools are on the table. He walks around the wood, terrified. He does not want to touch it. He knows that he must. But he does not want to defile the wood. He stares and stares, almost weeping. He wishes that the wood would speak to him; he is waiting for the wood to speak. Until it speaks, he cannot move. I am imprisoned somewhere in the silence of that wood, and so is he.

He picks up a chisel, he puts it down. He lights a cigarette, sits down on his work stool, stares, picks up the chisel again.

He puts it down, goes into the kitchen to pour himself a beer, comes back with the beer, sits down on the stool again, stares at the wood. The wood stares back at him.

"You cunt," says Fonny.

He picks up the chisel again, and approaches the waiting wood. He touches it very lightly with his hand, he caresses it. He listens. He puts the chisel, teasingly, against it. The chisel begins to move. Fonny begins.

And wakes up.

He is in a cell by himself, at the top of the prison. This is provisional. Soon, he will be sent downstairs, to a larger cell, with other men. There is a toilet in the corner of the cell. It stinks.

And Fonny stinks.

He yawns, throwing his arms behind his head, and turns, furiously, on the narrow cot. He listens. He cannot tell what time it is, but it does not matter. The hours are all the same, the days are all the same. He looks at his shoes, which have no laces, on the floor beside the cot. He tries to give himself some reason for being here, some reason to move, or not to move. He knows that he must do something to keep himself from drowning in this place, and every day he tries. But he does not succeed. He can neither retreat into himself nor step out of himself. He is righteously suspended, he is still. He is still with fear. He rises, and walks to the corner, and pees. The toilet does not work very well, soon it will overflow. He does not know what he can do about it. He is afraid, up here, alone. But he is also afraid of the moment when he will be moved downstairs, with the others, whom he sees at mealtimes, who see him. He knows who they are, he has seen them all before, were they to encounter each other outside he would know what to say to them. Here, he knows nothing, he is dumb, he is absolutely terrified. Here, he is at everyone's mercy, and he is also at the mercy of this stone and steel. Outside, he is not young.

Here, he realizes that he is young, very young, too young. And—will he grow old here?

He stares through the small opening in the cell door into what he can see of the corridor. Everything is still and silent. It must be very early. He wonders if today is the day he will be taken to the showers. But he does not know what day it is, he cannot remember how long ago it was that he was taken to the showers. I'll ask somebody today, he thinks, and then I'll remember. I've got to make myself remember. I can't let myself go like this. He tries to remember everything he has ever read about life in prison. He can remember nothing. His mind is as empty as a shell; rings, like a shell, with a meaningless sound, no questions, no answers, nothing. And he stinks. He yawns again, he scratches himself, he shivers, with a mighty effort he stifles a scream, grabs the bars of the high window and looks up into what he can see of the sky. The touch of the steel calms him a little; the cool, rough stone against his skin comforts him a little. He thinks of Frank, his father. He thinks of me. He wonders what we are doing now, at this very moment. He wonders what the whole world, his world, is doing without him, why he has been left alone here, perhaps to die. The sky is the color of the steel; the heavy tears drip down Fonny's face, causing the stubble on his face to itch. He cannot muster his defenses because he can give himself no reason for being here.

He lies back down on the cot. He has five cigarettes left. He knows that I will bring him cigarettes this evening. He lights a cigarette, staring up at the pipes on the ceiling. He shakes. He tries to put his mind at ease. *Just one more day. Don't sweat it. Be cool.*

He drags on the cigarette. His prick hardens. Absently, he strokes it, through his shorts; it is his only friend. He clenches his teeth, and resists, but he is young and he is lonely, he is alone. He strokes himself gently, as though in prayer, closing his eyes. His rigid sex responds, burning, and Fonny sighs, dragging on the cigarette again. He pauses, but his hand will not be still—cannot be still. He catches his lower lip in his teeth, wishing—but the hand will not be still. He lifts himself out of his shorts and pulls the blanket up to his chin. The hand will not be still, it tightens, it tightens, moving faster, and Fonny sinks and rises. Oh. He tries to think of no one, he tries not to think of me, he does not wish me to have any connection with this cell, or with this act. Oh. And he turns, rising, writhing, his belly beginning to shake. Oh: and great tears gather behind his eyes. He does not want it to end. It must end. Oh. Oh. Oh. He drops his cigarette on the stone floor, he surrenders totally, he pretends that human arms are holding him, he moans, he nearly screams, his thickening, burning sex causes him to arch his back, and his limbs stiffen. Oh. He does not want it to end. It must end. He moans. It is unbelievable. His sex trickles, spurts, explodes, all over his hand and his belly and his balls, he sighs; after a long moment he opens his eyes and the cell comes crashing down on him, steel and stone, making him know he is alone.

He is brought down to see me at six o'clock.

He remembers to pick up the phone.

"Hey!" And he grins. "How you doing, baby? Tell me something."

"You know I ain't got nothing to tell. How you?"

He kisses the glass. I kiss the glass.

But he does not look well.

"Hayward's coming to see you tomorrow morning. He thinks he's got a date fixed for the trial."

"For when?"

"Soon. Very soon."

"What do you mean by soon? Tomorrow? Next month? Next year?"

"Would I tell you, Fonny, if I didn't know it was soon? Would I? And Hayward *told* me I could tell you."

"Before the baby gets here?"

"Oh, yes, before the baby gets here."

"When is it due?"

"Soon."

His face changes then, and he laughs. He makes a mock menacing gesture with one fist.

"How is it? the baby."

"Alive and kicking. Believe me."

"Whipping your ass, huh?" He laughs again. "Old Tish."

And again his face changes, another light comes into it, he is very beautiful.

"You seen Frank?"

"Yes. He's been doing a lot of overtime. He'll be here tomorrow."

"He coming with you?"

"No. He's coming with Hayward, in the morning."

"How is he?"

"He's fine, baby."

"And my two funky sisters?"

"They're like they've always been."

"Not married yet?"

"No, Fonny. Not yet."

I wait for the next question:

"And my Mama?"

"I haven't seen her. Naturally. But she seems to be all right."

"Her weak heart ain't done her in yet, huh? Your Mama back from Puerto Rico?"

"Not yet. But we expect her any minute."

His face changes again.

"But—if that chick still says I raped her—I'm going to be here for a while."

I light a cigarette, and I put it out. The baby moves, as though it is trying to get a glimpse of Fonny.

"Mama thinks that Hayward can destroy her testimony. She seems to be a kind of hysterical woman. She's a part-time whore, anyway—that doesn't help her case. And—you were the blackest thing in the lineup that morning. There were some white cats and a Puerto Rican and a couple of light brown brothers—but you were the only *black* man."

"I don't know how much that's going to mean."

"Well, one thing it *can* mean is that the case can be thrown out of court. She says she was raped by a black man, and so they put *one* black man in a lineup with a whole lot of pale dudes. And so, naturally, she says it was you. If she was looking for a black cat, she *knows* it can't be none of the others."

"What about Bell?"

"Well, he's already killed one black kid, just like I told you. And Hayward will make sure that the jury knows that."

"Shit. If the jury knows that, they'll probably want to give him a medal. He's keeping the streets safe."

"Fonny, don't think like that. Baby. We agreed when this shit started, that we'd just have to move it from day to day and not blow our cool and not try to think too far ahead. I know exactly what you mean, sweetheart, but there's no point in thinking about it like that——"

"Do you miss me?"

"Oh, God, yes. That's why you can't blow your cool. I'm waiting for you, the baby's waiting for you!"

"I'm sorry, Tish. I'm sorry. I'll get it together. I really will. But, sometimes it's hard, because I ain't got no business here—you know? And things are happening inside me that I don't really understand, like I'm beginning to see things I never saw before. I don't have any words for those things, and I'm scared. I'm not as tough as I thought I was. I'm younger than I thought I was. But I'll get it together. I promise you. I promise. Tish. I'll be better when I come out than I was when I came in. I promise. I know it. Tish. Maybe there's something I had to see, and—I couldn't have seen it without coming in here. Maybe. Maybe that's it. Oh, Tish—do you love me?"

"I love you. I love you. You *have* to know I love you, just like you know that nappy hair is growing on your head."

"Do I look awful?"

"Well, I wish I could get my hands on you. But you're beautiful to me."

"I wish I could get my hands on you, too."

A silence falls, and we look at each other. We are looking at each other when the door opens behind Fonny, and the man appears. This is always the most awful moment, when Fonny has to rise and turn, I have to rise and turn. But Fonny is cool. He stands, and raises his fist. He smiles, and stands there for a moment, looking me dead in the eye. Something travels from him to me, it is love and courage. Yes. Yes. We are going to make it, somehow. Somehow. I stand, and smile, and raise my fist. He turns into the inferno. I walk toward the Sahara.

The miscalculations of this world are vast. The D.A.'s office, the prosecution, the state—*The People versus Alonzo Hunt!*—has managed to immobilize, isolate, or intimidate, every witness for Alonzo Hunt. But it has fucked itself up, too, as a thinned Sharon informs us on the night that Ernestine borrows the actress's car, and chauffeur, to bring Mama home from Kennedy Airport:

"I waited for another two days. I thought, it can't go down like that. The deal can *not* go down like that. Jaime said that it could, it *would* go down like that. By this time, the story was all over the island. Everybody knew it. Jaime knew more about it than I knew myself. He said that I was being followed everywhere, that *we* were being followed everywhere, and, one night, in the taxi, he proved it. I'll tell you about that another day."

Mama's face: she, too, is seeing something she never saw before.

"I couldn't go around anymore. For the last two days, Jaime got to be my spy, really. They knew his taxi better than they knew him, if you see what I mean. People always know the outside better than they know the inside. If they saw Jaime's taxi coming, well, that was Jaime. They didn't look inside."

Sharon's face: and Joseph's face.

"So, he borrowed somebody else's car. That way, they didn't see him coming. By the time they *did* see him, it didn't make any difference, since he wasn't with me. He was part of the landscape, like the sea, like the garbage heap, he was something they had known all their lives. They didn't have to look at him. I had never seen it like that before. Maybe they didn't *dare* look at him, like they don't look at the garbage dump. Like they don't look at themselves—like *we* don't look. I had never seen it like that before. Never. I don't speak no Spanish and they don't speak no English. But we on the same garbage dump. For the same reason."

She looks at me.

"For the same reason. I had never thought about it like that before. Who*ever* discovered America *deserved* to be dragged home, in chains, to die."

She looks at me again.

"You get that baby here, you hear me?" And she smiles. She smiles. She is very close to me. And she is very far away. "We ain't going to let nobody put chains on that baby. That's all."

She rises, and paces the kitchen. We watch her: she *has* lost weight. She holds a gin and orange juice in her hand. I know that she has not yet unpacked. I realize, because I watch her fighting her tears, that she is, really, after all, young.

"Anyway. He was there, Jaime was there, when they carried the chick away. She was screaming. She was having a miscarriage. Pietro carried her down the steps, in his arms. She had already started to bleed."

She sips her drink. She stands at our window, very much alone.

"She was carried to the mountains, someplace called *Barranguitas*. You got to know where it is, to get there. Jaime says that she will never be seen again."

There goes the trial, the prosecution having fucked itself out of its principal witness. We have a slim hope, still, in Daniel, but not one of us can see him, even if we knew where he could be found. He has been transferred to a prison upstate: Hayward is checking it out, Hayward is on the case.

The prosecution will ask for time. We will ask that the charge be dropped, and the case dismissed: but must be prepared to settle for bail: if the state will concede it: if we can raise it.

"All right," says Joseph, stands, walks to the window,

stands next to Sharon, but does not touch her. They watch their island.

"You okay?" asks Joseph, and lights a cigarette, and hands it to her.

"Yeah. I'm okay."

"Then, let's go on in. You tired. And you been gone a while."

"Good-night," says Ernestine, firmly, and Sharon and Joseph, their arms around each other, walk down the hall, to their room. In a way, *we* are their elders now. And the baby kicks again. Time.

But the effect of all this on Frank is cataclysmic, is absolutely disastrous, and it is Joseph who has to bring him the news. Their hours are, furthermore, now so erratic that he has to bring the news to the house.

Without a word, he has managed to forbid both Ernestine and myself from saying a word to the Hunts.

It is about midnight.

Mrs. Hunt is in bed. Adrienne and Sheila have just come in, and, standing in the kitchen, in their nightgowns, are giggling and sipping Ovaltine. Adrienne's behind is spreading, but there is no hope for Sheila at all. Sheila has been told that she resembles a nothing actress, Merle Oberon, whom she has encountered on the Late Late Show, and so she has clipped her eyebrows with the same intention, but not to the same effect. The Oberon chick was paid, at least, for her disquieting resemblance to an egg.

Joseph must be on the docks in the early morning,

and so he has no time to waste. Neither does Frank, who must also be downtown, early.

Frank puts a beer before Joseph, pours a little wine for himself. Joseph takes a sip of his beer. Frank sips his wine. They watch each other for a rather awful moment, aware of the girls' laughter in the kitchen. Frank wants to make the laughter stop, but he cannot take his eyes from Joseph's eyes.

"Well—?" says Frank.

"Brace yourself. I'm going to hit you hard. The trial's been postponed because the Puerto Rican chick, dig, has lost her baby and look like she's flipped her wig, too, lost her mind, man, anyway she in the hills of Puerto Rico someplace and she can't be moved and can't nobody see her, she can't come to New York now, no *way* and so the City wants the trial postponed—until she *can*." Frank says nothing. Joseph says, "You understand what I'm saying?"

Frank sips his wine, and says, quietly, "Yeah. I understand."

They hear the girls' low voices in the kitchen: this sound is about to drive both men insane.

Frank says, "You telling me that they going to keep Fonny in jail until this chick comes to her senses." He sips his wine again, looks at Joseph. "Is that right?"

Something in Frank's aspect is beginning to terrify Joseph, but he does not know what it is.

"Well—that's what they *want* to do. But we might be able to get him out, on bail."

Frank says nothing. The girls giggle, in the kitchen.

"How much bail?"

"We don't know. It ain't been set yet." He sips his beer, more and more frightened, obscurely, but profoundly.

"When is it going to be set?"

"Tomorrow. The day after." He has to say it: "If—"

"If what?"

"If they accept our plea, man. They ain't *got* to let us have no bail." There is something else he has to say. "And—I don't think this will happen, but it's better to look at it from the *worst* side—they *might* try to make the charge against Fonny heavier because the chick's lost her baby, and seems to have flipped her wig."

Silence: the girlish laughter from the kitchen.

Joseph scratches one armpit, watching Frank. Joseph is more and more uneasy.

"So," says Frank, finally, with an icy tranquility, "we're fucked."

"What makes you say that, man? It's rough, I agree, but it ain't yet over."

"Oh, *yes*," says Frank, "it's over. They got him. They ain't going to let him go till they get ready. And they ain't ready yet. And ain't nothing we can do about it."

Joseph shouts, out of his fear, "We *got* to do something about it!" He hears his voice, banging against the walls, against the girlish laughter from the kitchen.

"What can we do about it?"

"If they give us bail, get the change together—"

"How?"

"Man, I don't know how! I just know we have to do it!"

"And if they don't give us bail?"

"We get him *out!* I don't care what we have to do to get him out!"

"I don't, neither! But what can we *do?*"

"*Get him out.* That's what we have to do. We both know he ain't *got* no business in there. Them lying motherfuckers, they know it, too." He stands. He is trembling. The kitchen is silent. "Look. I know what you're saying. You're saying they got us by the balls. Okay. But that's our flesh and blood, baby: *our flesh and blood.* I don't know *how* we going to do it. I just know we have to do it. I know you ain't scared for you, and God knows I ain't scared for me. That boy is got to come out of there. That's all. And we got to get him out. That's all. And the first thing we got to do, man, is just not to lose our nerve. We can't let these cunt-faced white-assed motherfuckers get away with this shit no longer." He subsides, he sips his beer. "They been killing our children long enough."

Frank looks toward the open kitchen door, where his two daughters stand.

"Is everything all right?" Adrienne asks.

Frank hurls his glass of wine onto the floor, it rings and shatters. "You two dizzy off-white cunts, get the fuck out of my face, you hear? *Get the fuck out of my face.* If you was any kind of women you'd be peddling pussy on the block to get your brother out of jail instead of giving it away for free to all them half-assed faggots who come sniffing around you with a book under their arm. Go to bed! *Get out of my face!*"

Joseph watches the daughters. He sees something very strange, something he had never thought of: he sees that Adrienne loves her father with a really desperate love. She knows he is in pain. She would soothe it if she could, she does not know how. She would give anything to know how. She does not know that she reminds Frank of her mother.

Without a word, she drops her eyes and turns away, and Sheila follows her.

The silence is enormous—it spreads and spreads. Frank puts his head in his hands. Then, Joseph sees that Frank loves his daughters.

Frank says nothing. Tears drop onto the table, trickling down from the palms with which he has covered his face. Joseph watches: the tears drip from the palm, onto the wristbone, to splash—with a light, light, intolerable sound—on the table. Joseph does not know what to say —yet:

"This ain't no time for crying, man," he says. He finishes his beer. He watches Frank. "You all right?"

Frank says, finally, "Yeah. I'm all right."

Joseph says, "Get some sleep. We got to move it early in the morning. I'll talk to you end of the day. You got it?"

"Yeah," says Frank. "I got it."

When Fonny learns that the trial has been postponed, and learns why, and what effect Victoria's disaster may have on his own—it is I who tell him—something quite strange, altogether wonderful, happens in him. It is not that he gives up hope, but that he ceases clinging to it.

"Okay," is all he says.

I seem to see his high cheekbones for the first time, and perhaps this is really true, he has lost so much weight. He looks straight at me, into me. His eyes are enormous, deep and dark. I am both relieved and frightened. He has moved—not away from me: but he has moved. He is standing in a place where I am not.

And he asks me, staring at me with those charged, enormous eyes,

"You all right?"

"Yes. I'm all right."

"The baby all right?"

"Yes. The baby's fine."

He grins. It is, somehow, a shock. I will always see the space where the missing tooth has been.

"Well. I'm all right, too. Don't you worry. I'm coming home. I'm coming home, to you. I want you in my arms. I want your arms around me. I've got to hold our baby in my arms. It's got to be. You keep the faith."

He grins again, and everything inside me moves. Oh, love. Love.

"Don't you worry. I'll be home."

He grins again, and stands, and salutes me. He looks at me, hard, with a look I have never seen on any face before. He touches himself, briefly, he bends to kiss the glass, I kiss the glass.

Now, Fonny knows why he is here—why he is where he is; now, he dares to look around him. He is not here for anything he has done. He has always known that, but now he knows it with a difference. At meals, in the showers, up and down the stairs, in the evening, just before everyone is locked in again, he looks at the others, he listens: what have *they* done? Not much. To do much is to have the power to place these people where they are, and keep them where they are. These captive men are the hidden price for a hidden lie: the righteous must be able to locate the damned. To do much is to have the power and the necessity to dictate to the damned. But that, thinks Fonny, works both ways. *You're in or you're out. Okay. I see. Motherfuckers. You won't hang me.*

I bring him books, and he reads. We manage to get him paper, and he sketches. Now that he knows where he is, he begins to talk to the men, making himself, so to speak, at home. He knows that anything may happen to him here. But, since he knows it, he can no longer turn his back: he has to face it, even taunt it, play with it, dare.

He is placed in solitary for refusing to be raped. He loses a tooth, again, and almost loses an eye. Something hardens in him, something changes forever, his tears freeze in his belly. But he has leaped from the promontory of despair. He is fighting for his life. He sees his baby's face before him, he has an appointment he must keep, and he will be here, he swears it, sitting in the shit, sweating and stinking, when the baby gets here.

Hayward arranges the possibility of bail for Fonny. But it is high. And here comes the summer: time.

On a day that I will never forget, Pedrocito drove me home from the Spanish restaurant, and, heavy, heavy, heavy, I got to my chair and I sat down.

The baby was restless, and I was scared. It was almost time. I was so tired, I almost wanted to die. For a long time, because he was in solitary, I had not been able to see Fonny. I had seen him on this day. He was so skinny; he was so bruised: I almost cried out. To whom, where? I saw this question in Fonny's enormous, slanted black eyes—eyes that burned, now, like the eyes of a prophet. Yet, when he grinned, I saw, all over again, my lover, as though for the first time.

"We got to get some meat on your bones," I said. "Lord, have mercy."

"Speak up. He can't hear you." But he said it with a smile.

"We almost got the money to bail you out."

"I figured you would."

We sat, and we just looked at each other. We were making love to each other through all that glass and stone and steel.

"Listen, I'll soon be out. I'm coming home because I'm glad I came, can you dig that?"

I watched his eyes.

"Yes," I said.

"*Now*. I'm an artisan," he said. "Like a cat who makes —tables. I don't like the word artist. Maybe I never did.

I sure the fuck don't know what it means. I'm a cat who works from his balls, with his hand. I know what it's about now. I think I really do. Even if I go under. But I don't think I will. Now."

He is very far from me. He is with me, but he is very far away. And now he always will be.

"Where you lead me," I said, "I'll follow."

He laughed. "Baby. Baby. Baby. I love you. And I'm going to *build* us a table and a whole lot of folks going to be eating off it for a long, *long* time to come."

From my chair, I looked out my window, over these dreadful streets.

The baby asked,

Is there not one righteous among them?

And kicked, but with a tremendous difference, and I knew that my time was almost on me. I remember that I looked at my watch: it was twenty to eight. I was alone, but I knew that someone, soon, would be coming through the door. The baby kicked again, and I caught my breath, and I almost cried, and the phone rang.

I crossed the room, heavy, heavy, heavy, and I picked it up.

"Hello—?"

"Hello—Tish? This is Adrienne."

"How are you, Adrienne?"

"Tish—have you seen my father? Is Frank there?"

Her voice almost knocked me down. I had never heard such terror.

"No. Why?"

"When did you see him last?"

"Why—I *haven't* seen him. I know he's seen Joseph. But *I* haven't seen him."

Adrienne was weeping. It sounded horrible over the phone.

"Adrienne! What's the matter? What's the *matter?*"

And I remember that at that moment everything stood still. The sun didn't move and the earth didn't move, the sky stared down, waiting, and I put my hand on my heart to make it start beating again.

"Adrienne! *Adrienne!*"

"Tish—my Daddy was fired from his job, two days ago—they said he was stealing, and they threatened to put him in jail—and he was all upset, because of Fonny and all, and he was drunk when he came home and he cursed everybody out and then he went out the door and ain't nobody seen him since—Tish—don't you know where my father is?"

"Adrienne, baby, I don't. I swear to God, I don't. I haven't seen him."

"Tish, I know you don't like me——"

"Adrienne, you and me, we had a little fight, but that's all right. That's normal. That don't mean I don't like you. I would surely never do anything to hurt you. You're Fonny's *sister*. And if I love him, I *got* to love you. Adrienne—?"

"If you see him—will you call me?"

"Yes. Yes. Yes, of course."

"Please. Please. Please. I'm scared," said Adrienne, in a low, different altogether tone of voice, and she hung up.

I put down the phone and the key turned in the lock and Mama came in.

"Tish, what's the matter with you?"

I got back to my chair and I sat down in it.

"That was Adrienne. She's looking for Frank. She said that he was fired from his job, and that he was real upset. And Adrienne—that poor child sounds like she's gone to pieces. Mama"—and we stared at each other; my mother's face was as still as the sky—"has Daddy seen him?"

"I don't know. But Frank ain't been by here."

She put her bag down on top of the TV set and came over and put her hand on my brow.

"How you feeling?"

"Tired. Funny."

"You want me to get you a little brandy?"

"Yes. Thank you, Mama. That might be a good idea. It might help to settle my stomach."

She went into the kitchen and came back with the brandy and put it in my hand.

"Your stomach upset?"

"A little. It'll go away."

I sipped the brandy, and I watched the sky. She watched me for a moment, then she went away again. I watched the sky. It was as though it had something to say to me. I was in some strange place, alone. Everything was still. Even the baby was still.

Sharon came back.

"You see Fonny today?"

"Yes."

"And how was he?"

"He's beautiful. They beat him up, but they didn't beat him—if you see what I mean. He's beautiful."

But I was so tired, I remember that I could hardly speak. Something was about to happen to me. That was what I felt, sitting in that chair, watching the sky—and I couldn't move. All I could do was wait.

Until my change comes.

"I think Ernestine's got the rest of the money," Sharon said, and smiled. "From her actress."

Before I could say anything, the doorbell rang, and Sharon went to the door. Something in her voice, at the door, made me stand straight up and I dropped the brandy glass on the floor. I still remember Sharon's face, she was standing behind my father, and I remember my father's face.

Frank had been found, he told us, way, way, way up the river, in the woods, sitting in his car, with the doors locked, and the motor running.

I sat down in my chair.

"Does Fonny know?"

"I don't think so. Not yet. He won't know till morning."

"I've got to tell him."

"You can't get there till morning, daughter."

Joseph sat down.

Sharon asked me, sharply, "How you feeling, Tish?"

I opened my mouth to say—I don't know what. When I opened my mouth, I couldn't catch my breath. Everything disappeared, except my mother's eyes. An incredible intelligence charged the air between us. Then, all I could see was Fonny. And then I screamed, and my time had come.

Fonny is working on the wood, on the stone, whistling, smiling. And, from far away, but coming nearer, the baby cries and cries and cries and cries and cries and cries and cries and cries, cries like it means to wake the dead.

[Columbus Day] Oct. 12, 1973
St. Paul de Vence